THE RECONCILER:
Paid in Full

Anthony DiCristofano

ISBN: 979-8-9995181-4-9

TABLE OF CONTENTS

Prologue: Vlad's Hospoda (Berwyn, 1984)

The screams had been going on for almost three minutes.

Not the kind that rise and fall. These were jagged, ragged, the raw edge of a voice unraveling in real time. Someone was being taken apart behind that door, and it wasn't going quickly.

Out in the main room of Vlad's Hospoda, no one turned.

The ceiling fan ticked uselessly overhead, slicing the cigarette haze into lazy ribbons. Poker machines blinked in the corner like forgotten Christmas lights. A black-and-white television bolted above the bar played WGN News at low volume, Len O'Connor mumbling about the city budget while a banner crawled about CTA service cuts.

A barback, young, too clean, maybe new, glanced toward the hall. Nobody met his eyes. One of the older men at the rail bumped the TV volume up a notch with the remote. Another sipped Old Style. Another slowly chewed a wedge of kielbasa.

A minute passed like that. Maybe more. Then the hallway door opened.

He stepped out with that walk, the one that made your gut clench.

The body moved, but not as one piece. Heaving first to one side, then the other. The right leg glided forward with almost unnatural smoothness, but the left came down hard, a mechanical clunk that landed flat and final. The left shoe was built up at least three inches, wrapped in matte black leather like a large hoof. The weight of it bent his gait into a listing sway, hips tilting unnaturally.

His arms didn't swing right, either. Locked at the elbows, they moved from the shoulders like poorly wired limbs on a bad puppet. The torso shifted out of rhythm with the legs, as if gravity had different instructions for each section. There was no cadence to it. No rhythm. Just motion, jerking and staggered, a dysfunctional marionette doing his best imitation of normal.

Some called him Big Shoe. Some didn't call him anything at all.

He wore the same brown suit as always, decades out of fashion even for Eastern Europe. Wide lapels, the color of old funeral curtains. The fabric held sharp creases but didn't drape right on his frame. His shoulder line was uneven, one side hiked awkwardly higher. The beige shirt underneath had a faint ring of salt where the collar met skin. His tie, a dull burgundy, patterned with tiny squares, was knotted too tight, like it had been tied once in 1969 and never undone.

In his right hand, a thick white handkerchief stained at one edge. In the left, a heavy steel fork. The kind with three thick tines. The kind you didn't find in restaurants. The kind that glinted with something dark and wet at the tips.

He paused in the doorway. Took a slow breath. Dotted his forehead with the cloth.

2

Then, turning gently back toward the hallway, he spoke in a voice that almost didn't match the rest of him. Calm. Clipped. Eastern accent cut with Chicago vowels:

"I'll see you next veek."

The door creaked shut behind him.

He began his slow passage through the bar. His built-up shoe clunked with each step. No one flinched. One of the old men nodded, subtle as a bow. Another shifted his gaze to the poker machine.

Big Shoe returned the nod. Almost warm. Then raised the handkerchief and delicately wiped the fork clean. He held it at eye level, studied the curve of the tines, like a craftsman admiring his tool. The rag folded, once, twice. The fork disappeared into an inside coat pocket.

At the door, he paused again. Looked back toward the bar, his right eye sharp and glassy beneath thick lenses. The left one, cloudy and pale, didn't track. Just stared.

Then he turned.

The door eased shut behind him.

Silence.

Eventually, the barback, maybe 21, maybe not, slid off his stool and crept down the hall. The others let him. Let him learn.

He stopped at the back room door. It was unlocked. Slightly ajar.

He pushed it open with the edge of his sneaker.

The light inside buzzed, one bulb out, the other flickering. A single wooden chair lay on its side, legs twisted. Blood pooled beneath it in slow syrupy coils. A man lay twisted near the corner, curled like a dead insect. Breathing, barely. Fingers, three of them, sat carefully arranged on the table beside him. Like place settings. One of the severed digits still bore a wedding ring.

The barback blinked. Closed the door. Turned the bolt.

When he came back, no one asked what he saw. He sat at the edge of the bar and stared straight ahead, jaw slightly slack, hands loose in his lap.

WGN played on.

Somewhere behind the walls, the furnace kicked on with a rattle.

Outside, the night was still. But if you listened closely, you could hear it. The sound of a man walking east on 22nd Street. A staccato rhythm no one could ever quite replicate.

Clunk.

Pause.

Glide.

Pause.

Clunk.

Chapter 1: The Pizzeria (Cicero, 1984)

It sat on the corner like it always had, not asking for attention, not needing any. A low, square building of clean brick and modest pride. The awning above the entrance was deep green canvas, no branding, no slogan. Just three stitched words near the hem in cursive white: **Dal 1956.** If you knew what that meant, you were halfway in. If you didn't, you kept walking.

The sidewalk out front was always swept. Not by the city, by someone who worked inside. Clean edges. No weeds. No loose trash. You wouldn't find gum wrappers or busted bottles here. The windows were half-covered in white lace curtains, nothing decorative, just enough to keep eyes from wandering. You could see the top of the wine rack through the glass. Nothing else.

No posted menu. No business hours. No plastic decals for credit cards. Just a brass plaque screwed into the doorframe at chest level that read:
CASH ONLY.
And beside it, a small black mailbox. Locked, unmarked.

The door was dark-stained oak with a brass handle, polished by time and repetition. A bell wired above it rang sharp when opened, no chime, no beep. Just a hard metallic ping, like the beginning of a warning.

Across the street sat the **hotel bar**, though calling it a hotel was generous. A narrow building with paint chipping at the corners and four thin windows that looked more like excuses than shelter. Beneath it, a bar that didn't bother with signage. It served two kinds of people: the ones already drunk, and the ones on their way to lose the rest at **Hawthorne Race Track**.

Men loitered out front during daylight hours, leaning on newspaper boxes, chewing toothpicks, arguing about late scratches. Paper racing forms in hand, hair slicked back with cheap product, sunglasses worn whether or not the sun was out. Some days they looked like they hadn't been inside since Tuesday.

Inside the bar, there was a woman behind the counter, heavy, middle-aged, not shy about her roots. Wore cutoff sleeves, spoke in a voice carved out of sandpaper and smoke. Locals called her "Georgia," though no one was sure if that was her name or just where she came from. She had one particular skill: she could throw an empty beer bottle across the full length of the bar into the garbage with perfect speed and precision, without ever breaking conversation. Like it was part of her nervous system.

The building was tired, but alive, propped up by bad decisions and cheap liquor. Some said it had mob ties too, once. Others said it was where the Anton Hotel sent guests who overstayed their welcome. The Anton was just around the corner, still open, still standing, but aging fast. Its lights flickered at night like they were forgetting how.

But the pizzeria didn't flicker.
It didn't creak or sag or shuffle.

It sat there, clean, unadorned, untouched by the sag around it.

In the shadows of the dying Hawthorne Works, its abandoned tower rising like the turret of a defeated castle, you could walk past the bust outs from Hawthorne Race Track, drunk, broke, racing form still crumpled in their hands, hear a scream from the flophouse bar, see a patrol car creep by slow with the window cracked, and none of it mattered.

Because behind that oak door, the air was cold, the rules were quiet, and the only heat came from the oven or the names in the envelopes.

Chapter 2: Inside the Pizzeria

The bell snapped sharp as the door opened, a metallic *ping* that cut the air clean and brief.

The light inside was low by design. Even on a bright day, the room stayed dim, lit by five old pendant lamps hanging in a line over the booths, each one fitted with a low-watt bulb behind yellowed glass. The shadows weren't heavy, just *permanent*. The kind that suggested privacy, not secrecy. You could see what you needed to. Nothing more.

The smell hit right as the door shut, garlic, yeast, tomato, and flour scorched where it touched the stone. No gimmicks, no perfume. Just the smell of food done right. You could smell the dough before you saw it, rising slow in the back. Oil clung to the air.

The floor was narrow black-and-white tile, faded and worn smooth in two paths: one from the front door to the register, and one that led to the back hallway, where you didn't go unless you were asked to. The booths were built like fortresses: thick iron pedestals bolted through the tile, tabletops that didn't wobble. The seats were old-school vinyl, dark red with metallic flecks that caught the light just so. Rounded backs, high and firm, trimmed in chrome. They squeaked when you shifted and stuck a little in summer, but no one complained. They weren't meant to coddle. Just last.

Each table had a glass shaker of crushed red pepper, half-caked with use, and a sugar shaker that no one ever touched. The forks were heavy and cold. The plates were white with a single green ring, all from the same supplier, all chipped slightly at the rim.

Along the back wall, a hand-built shelf held unlabeled wine bottles, mostly Chianti, a few straw-bottomed jugs, a couple of dusty dark greens with handwritten paper slips rubber-banded to the necks. The espresso machine hissed softly behind the counter, chrome-faced, old, industrial. Cleaned every night. It didn't make froth; it made espresso, two at a time, bitter and small. If you asked for milk, you got a look.

The register was a solid brass NCR, the kind with pull levers and a number dial that spun like a roulette wheel. It still printed paper receipts. The drawer opened with a heavy *clang*, loud enough to hush a conversation. But no one raised their voice in here anyway.

There was a rhythm to the room, a constant low hum. Silverware clinked softly. Chairs scraped once and then stayed still. Nobody lingered by the door. You walked in, you sat down, you didn't look around unless you had a reason.

Behind the counter stood an older man with the shape of someone who'd worked with dough most of his life, broad forearms, belly low and hard like he'd carried flour sacks for years. He wore a white apron, clean, pressed, folded at the waist, and a collared shirt beneath. His hair was thin but groomed. On his bicep, a blurred tattoo of the Italian flag done freehand years ago in prison. He never wrote anything down. He didn't need to.

In the corner, near the back hallway, sat The Booth.

Red leather cushions, still intact. Slightly raised platform, not much, but enough to give a line of sight. The wall beside it was blank except for a small framed photo of two men shaking hands. One of them was Sinatra. The other wasn't smiling.

That booth didn't have a reserved sign. It didn't need one. People didn't sit there unless they were supposed to. And if they made the mistake once, they didn't make it twice.

The jukebox near the kitchen door still worked. Still lit. Still humming. That afternoon it played *Come Back to Sorrento*, the version with the strings that made old men go quiet. Nobody needed to feed it anymore, Lou handled that. A new track rolled every hour or so, always something Italian, always something familiar. Dean Martin. Louie Prima. A little Pavarotti if Gina was in the mood. It wasn't background noise. It was part of the room, like the tiled floor and the smell of espresso.

From the back hallway came the soft click of a door latch, then a voice low and unreadable. Someone passed through, nodded to the man at the counter, and disappeared out the front, no food, no receipt. Just a small envelope left behind on the brass ledge by the register. Nobody looked at it. It would be gone soon.

Chapter 3: The Booth

The older man sat in the corner booth, right side, back wall. Same spot every time. His name was Lou. No one called him Louie anymore.

He wore a light blue dress shirt, sleeves rolled once. Hair slicked straight back, streaked silver at the temples. No jewelry except a gold pinky ring, worn smooth. A short espresso cup sat in front of him, untouched but already cooling. He wasn't in a hurry. He never was.

Across from him sat the kid, late-twenties, jacket unzipped, a little too much energy in his shoulders. Name was Nicky. South Side transplant. Came up under Angelo's crew, now working out of Cicero for the time being. Eager to impress. Eager to prove.

Lou watched him, then tilted his chin toward the front door.

That sound again.

Clunk… soft… clunk.

They both looked.

He entered like he always did. Big Shoe. Brown suit, same as ever. Coat buttoned. Shirt pressed. Tie tight. The thick-rimmed glasses sat high on the bridge of his nose, the left lens catching the light, the eye behind it a foggy void. The other eye scanned, quick and hard. He moved like a man not in a rush, but not slow either.

The platform shoe hit the tile like punctuation.

He stepped to the counter. Slid a small envelope forward.

The man behind the counter nodded, handed him another. Big Shoe gave a soft bow.

"Zank you, sir," he said.

Then, almost too quiet to hear:

"Have ze pleasant day."

He turned and walked out, shoulders rocking slightly, gait lopsided but smooth. No one else in the place reacted. Just two more steps. **Clunk. Clunk.** Then the bell above the door rang once, and the light shifted.

Nicky leaned back and scoffed.

"Who's the weird Kraut?"

The words weren't loud, but they were enough.

"Oh!" Lou barked it sharp, the way Italians do when they're cutting you off. Both hands came up in the *ma che vuoi*. "Show some fuckin' respect."

The kid blinked. He wasn't used to being checked like that. He straightened up a little, the corner of his mouth tightening like maybe he'd misjudged the room.

Lou didn't wait for a response. He leaned in, voice lower now, not angry, just heavy.

"That guy is a serious contractor. You understand what I'm saying? A fuckin' machine. Vito found him sometime after the war. Put him to work. It's been history since."

Nicky glanced back toward the door. Big Shoe was already gone.

"But we got soldiers," he said, still a little defensive. "Why use a straniero?"

Lou didn't answer right away. He turned toward the counter.

"Gina," he called, "two espressos and a couple cannoli's, bella."

Then, to the kid:

"Sit down. I'm gonna educate your ignorant self."

***

Gina brought the espresso and cannoli without a word. She didn't ask who ordered. Just placed two cups and a narrow white plate between them, powdered sugar rising in a soft cloud before settling again.

Lou nodded once, polite, not warm. She returned to the counter. No small talk. Not in this booth.

Nicky shifted in his seat. He tried to sit like he didn't care, but the movement betrayed him, too quick, too straight. He picked up his espresso but didn't drink. Lou didn't reach for his either.

There was a silence between them now. Not the lazy kind. The kind that **waited for correction**.

Lou's hands were steady. He stirred his espresso once, clockwise, with the little spoon. The sound of metal on porcelain echoed sharper than expected. Then he set the spoon down and looked across the table.

"You got a mouth on you, Nicky," he said, not harsh, just stating it.

Nicky gave a small shrug, trying to recover his footing.

"I didn't mean nothing by it."

Lou nodded, slow.

"Yeah, you did. You meant *you didn't know who that was.*"

A beat passed. Nicky lowered his eyes.

Lou leaned in slightly, voice low but clean.

"That man you just laughed at? He's not somebody's cousin doing collections on the side. He's not muscle. He's not crew. He's not even *like us*. He's something else."

He was now tapping his index and middle fingers of his right hand on the tabletop in succession to make his point.

"You know what a contractor is, Nicky?"

The kid looked up, cautious now. "You mean… like, freelance?"

"No," Lou said. "I mean **deliberate**. I mean he doesn't show up unless somebody somewhere has already decided: 'This needs to be resolved.' And I mean resolved."

Lou picked up his espresso, took a sip, and set it down.

"He don't argue. He don't yell. He don't bring backup. He shows up, and when he walks out, the problem's changed shape."

***

16

Lou reached for a cannoli but didn't eat it. He just held it, like the story might spoil his appetite.

"You're used to guys who punch when they're mad. Guys who shout. Who throw bottles or swing a bat when someone disrespects 'em. That's not him."

He shook his head, not in disgust, in quiet correction.

Lou gave a dry chuckle, but there was no humor in it. "You know how we are, Nicky. Us Italians, we run hot. Everything's personal. We shout, we cry, we throw punches when we're mad, and we hug just as hard when we're not. That fire? It drives a lot of things. Loyalty, love, even the viciousness. But it's a double-edged thing. Gets you in trouble, makes you sloppy, makes you *feel* too much when you should be thinkin'."

He tapped his temple.

"That's where he's different. He's got none of that. No fire, no warmth. No reaction. He don't shout, don't curse, don't gloat. He just operates. Cold. Clean. Like he's got no stake in it at all."

Lou looked past Nicky for a moment, like the image of Big Shoe was floating there.

"Honestly? Gives me the fuckin' creeps. I've been around a lotta tough guys. Seen real monsters. But this one? He ain't like the rest. There's no hatred in him, no love either. Just… function."

He paused, leaned back slightly.

"And here's the thing, that's *exactly* why he's a blessing.

You send in a hothead, you get drama. You get blood, sure, but you also get stories, leaks, heat. But him?"

Lou shook his head once, slowly.

"He don't leave a mess. He don't miss. He don't ask questions. He's the blade, not the butcher. You don't send him because you want fear, you send him because you want quiet results."

Nicky leaned forward a little, watching now. Lou continued.

"I heard Vito picked him up sometime after the war. No one's sure where. Maybe Hungary, maybe Czechoslovakia. Maybe the East just let go of him and he drifted west."

He took another sip of espresso.

"There are rumors. People say he worked under doctors during the war, German, Russian, depends who's talking. Some say he was a medic. Others say he cut men open and made notes while they screamed."

"Someone said he even worked as a liaison with the Japanese on some project or unit....7......731 or something."

He didn't blink.

"I don't know what's true. But whatever he learned, it wasn't first aid. He's got a surgeon's hands, but he doesn't put you back together."

A silence stretched between them, like a cloth being pulled tight.

"He takes you apart."

Nicky's posture changed. Slight. Instinctual. Like his spine wanted to shrink into the booth.

Lou finally put the cannoli down, untouched.

"He used to carry a full roll — blades, clamps, bone tools. Over time, he cut it down. Now he's got a few instruments he trusts. Fork. Ice pick, sometimes pruning shears. That's it."

Lou looked down at the table.

"You don't need a whole set when you know what you're doing. You don't need backup when the job always gets done."

Nicky cleared his throat but didn't speak.

Lou continued, quiet now.

"He's efficient. He's relentless. Not flashy. Not cruel. Just final."

Lou reached for his espresso. He just held the tiny cup, thumb circling the rim like it helped him think.

"You ever see Mikey T's hand?"

Nicky blinked. "With the glove?"

Lou nodded slowly.

"Not a glove. Wraps it because the fingers are gone. Three of them. Right hand. Snapped off clean like celery. They say he didn't scream right away. Just sat there blinking while blood hit his shoes."

He took a short breath through his nose.

"He missed two payments. Lied about it. Tried to stall."

Lou finally drank. One sip.

"He's right-handed, by the way. Or he was."

Nicky looked like he wanted to ask something but didn't.

"Then there's Ziggy," Lou went on, setting the cup down with care. "Runs that greasy grill off Austin. Real mouthy prick. Started skimming from the poker machines, if you can believe it. Worse than that, he was talkin' shit, said he wasn't gonna pay a dime to any dirty degos."

He shook his head slowly.

"Word went around he got clipped in a car accident. But I know better. Shoe paid him a visit one night as he was closin' up. Next morning, they found him out back in the alley, sittin' in the garbage runoff like a broken doll. Blank fuckin' stare. Like he saw something that snapped his mind in half."

Lou leaned forward, voice even lower.

"Both shoulders — dislodged from the rotator cuffs. Like tearing parts off a cooked chicken. Tendons clipped. Kneecap popped loose like a bottle cap. But that ain't even the worst of it."

Nicky's brows drew in. "What do you mean?"

"He was touched," Lou said.

"Touched how?"

"Like… traumatized. He don't talk right no more. Just mumbles and drifts. Walks like his bones forgot how to hold him up. Stares at nothin'. Ain't just the body. It's like the Shoe hollowed him out from the inside."

He let it sit.

"Toast. Finito. That's what you're dealin' with here. This motherfucker ain't like the rest."

Lou gave a short shrug.

"He's got contacts." In Government, at the DMV, I don't know, but there's no hidin from dis guy. If someone disappears, he's da guy to call……he'll bring 'em back…..or at least a part of 'em for proof."

"He doesn't chase. He doesn't make threats. He just shows up. And when he does, there's nothing to negotiate. There's no speech."

He leaned in just a bit, voice low.

"He finds the weak spot and marks it. That's his way. Knee joint, shoulder socket, three fingers pressed against a counter. Whatever it is, he makes it speak."

Lou paused.

"And once it's done, he walks away like he just fixed something. Like he set a bone back into place."

Nicky sat back. His jaw worked silently for a moment.

"How does he know what to—"

Lou held up a finger.

"Don't. Don't try to figure that part out. That's the mistake people make. They put him under a microscope, and then it starts to fester. Some things, you don't get close to."

He tapped his temple lightly with the same finger.

"You want to keep this straight? Don't wonder how he thinks. Just know he gets results."

Lou leaned forward, voice lower now, not secretive, but serious in a way Nicky hadn't yet seen.

"I can see it clicked for you. Good. But don't get too curious."

Nicky stayed quiet.

"This ain't bedtime folklore, Nicky. It's not some crew tale you spin to scare new guys. You carry this one wrong, it marks you."

Lou tapped a thick knuckle on the table, slow and heavy.

"Don't talk about him with your friends. Don't joke. Don't repeat anything I said outside this room. Not even the tone. Got it?"

Nicky gave a short nod, but Lou didn't blink.

"I mean it. The less you say, the better. The less you *know*, even better than that. Don't start tryin' to piece him together, what makes him tick, where he learned the shit he does."

His hand hovered just above the table now, palm flat.

"I've seen guys do it. Start thinking they could learn from him."

He exhaled through his nose.

"This guy ain't some myth, Nicky. He's not a ghost. He's real. But he's not like the rest of us. He's what happens when the war don't end."

Nicky's jaw tightened a little.

Lou leaned in just an inch more.

"You want to stay sharp? Stay sane? Keep his name light in your mouth. Better yet, don't say it at all."

"This life of ours — good, bad, right wrong — it don't matter. It makes up who we are, me and you, a good portion of it anyway.

But we got other things outside of this world. Even if it's a small percentage, something that brings a smile. Maybe it's a pretty girl we spend time with. A fast car. A good glass of vino. Some braciole and mostaccioli on a Sunday. Whatever the fuck it is, it tells us we're alive. That life's worth living.

That motherfucker's got none of that. The only thing that keeps him going is bein' the machine. And the machine don't rust because it keeps moving, cold, unyielding, indifferent. He's got nothing that brings him pleasure. He's been dead for fuckin' years.

This is why I tell you — know it, understand it, but don't scrutinize it and most of all, don't repeat any of this. Capisce? This is a different motherfucker. Get it through your head."

Lou sat back. He picked up his coffee, took one slow sip, and set it down without looking at Nicky again.

From the kitchen door, the jukebox clicked and whirred. The first mournful notes of *Vesti La Giubba* floated out, Pavarotti's voice filling the room with a slow, aching rise that made the air feel heavier.

Nicky stared at the table's worn varnish, feeling the words settle in his gut.

He didn't need to ask any more questions.

Chapter 4: The Entrance

The door opened with a dry, weightless chime. Not loud. Not even noticeable at first. But Lou paused mid-sentence. His eyes flicked up, then down.

Nicky turned, and saw him.

Big Shoe.

He moved in a way that made you want to look away, not limping, not stumbling, but something in between, each step at odds with the last. He would heave one way, then the other, sometimes twice in the same stride, as if his balance shifted in slow, stubborn waves. One leg was shorter than the other, and the difference was bridged by a thick, three- or four-inch prosthetic shoe. Every time it came down, it made a sound unlike anything else on the street, not metallic, not quite wooden, but a hollow, resonant thud, like heavy bone striking an empty floor.

His arms never kept the same pace as his legs. Bent at the elbows but held stiff, they moved only from the shoulders, sometimes swinging forward in sync with the opposite leg, sometimes hanging away from his body in their own unpredictable rhythm. There was no pattern. At moments he leaned forward as if about to lunge, then straightened mid-step without reason. Other times his torso would sway in disagreement with his hips, the whole frame dragged slightly askew by some private gravity.

It was arrhythmic, a gait without cadence, without the symmetry the human eye expects. The movement disassembled itself as it happened, like a grotesque ballet performed in bad faith, each joint and limb refusing to agree on what came next. The more you watched, the worse it became, until the sight worked under your skin, leaving a residue of unease you couldn't shake. You didn't need to be told something was wrong. Your body already knew.

The suit was brown, but not the kind you'd find in an American department store. The fabric had a dull, heavy sheen, like it had been cut from outdated funeral curtains, something that belonged in a Czechoslovakian town hall in the 1960s. The cut was stiff and square, built for a frame that didn't match his own. The shoulders sat too high, the sleeves too short, the lines too rigid to move with him. It was pressed to an almost unnatural crispness, the creases sharp enough to look drawn on.

It was decades out of fashion, the kind of suit that had looked old even in the seventies, and by the eighties seemed like a relic that had slipped through the cracks of time. It carried the wrong history, not thrift-store old, not vintage, but foreign and unplaceable, like it had crossed an ocean without changing shape.

Beneath it, a beige-yellow shirt clung stiff at the collar. The fabric had the weary pallor of something washed too many times in hard water, its fibers tired but intact. At his throat sat a narrow tie, an outdated weave in a muted pattern, knotted perfectly in the center, but in a way that suggested it had been tied by someone else, long ago, and never truly undone. The knot had aged into place, as much a fixture as the man wearing it.

He wore it year-round, in all weather, even on the hottest days of July when the sidewalks of 22nd Street shimmered in the heat. While other men in Berwyn and Cicero shed jackets for short sleeves, he could be seen walking that stretch of pavement in the same brown suit, his gait slow, irregular, the heat pooling in the fabric. The air might be thick enough to make shirts stick to backs, but he never loosened the knot or rolled a cuff. The suit stayed neat. Immaculate. The kind of care you'd take with a uniform, not a personal choice.

On him, the ensemble looked neither formal nor casual, neither new nor antique, just wrong. The colors clashed with his pallor, and the fit pulled against his uneven frame, bunching in some places, gaping in others.

His glasses caught the light, one lens reflected clean. The other revealed a white cloud behind the glass, an eye fogged by some long-dead trauma. The good eye scanned the room, slow and sure.

Nicky froze. A hollow spread behind his ribs, the kind that comes right before instinct tells you to move. But he didn't. Couldn't. He just watched, silent.

The lighting overhead flickered slightly as Big Shoe passed under it, casting long shadows across his face. The hollows beneath his cheekbones deepened. His jaw sat slack, but not soft. He had the expression of a man walking to a job he'd done too many times to feel anything about.

He didn't stop at the table. Just clacked by, slow and steady, the limp creating a grotesque, silent rhythm that turned the floor into a stage. Like a broken ballet with no music, no applause. Just movement for its own sake.

As he passed, Nicky felt something shift in his chest. The man he'd called a "weird Kraut" just an hour ago, was something else now. Something colder. Something unbothered by recognition. Or consequence.

Big Shoe paused near the counter, handed off the envelope to Lou without a word, gave a small, precise nod, then turned. The clunk resumed.

Clunk. Step. Clunk. Step.

Nicky's eyes followed him all the way to the door. He didn't blink. Didn't breathe.

The door closed behind him.

Lou's mouth tugged slightly at one corner, not quite a smile, not quite a frown. Just a knowing crease. He looked back at Nicky and gave a slow, deliberate nod.

Nothing more needed to be said.

Chapter 5: The Daughter

He never held her.

Not when she was born in the ash-colored years after the war. Not when her newborn cry echoed through a maternity ward that smelled like antiseptic and steam. Not when her fingers curled reflexively toward the crook of a stranger's arm. There were no lullabies. No quiet nights rocked to sleep against a tired shoulder. No scent of talcum or sour milk on a father's collar.

She was his by blood, but never by presence. And presence, she would later say, is the only thing that truly raises a child.

War didn't part them with poetry. There was no noble sacrifice, no heartbreaking farewell. Her mother escaped west through crumbling streets and bartered silence, a forged passport tucked in her bra, a fake wedding band on her finger. He didn't chase her. He stayed behind, deeper in the system than anyone should be. There were corridors with locks, gurneys with leather straps, and cold rooms that didn't echo. He wore gloves. He signed papers. He vanished in a place where people didn't leave unless someone important decided they were no longer dangerous.

By the time he surfaced again in America, only a couple of years had passed. But her name had changed, and there was no place left for him.

Her mother worked long hours and spoke little about the past. When the topic veered toward the man in the old photos, if he even appeared at all, she would brush it off with something vague — "Just someone from a long time ago."

But to him, years earlier, she'd been direct: "Let her have a clean life."

So he kept his distance. Not because he wanted to, but because she had asked him to.

He watched instead.

From the rusted gate outside Saint Brigid's, coat collar raised, face turned sideways as children screamed into the wind at recess.

From the far side of the parking lot at her graduation, where folding chairs lined the lawn and mortarboards flew like startled crows.

From across the street as she moved into her first apartment, trying to carry a suitcase and a box of books in the same arm.

She was already her own person by then, not hardened, exactly, but settled. Grounded in the life her mother had built: a modest apartment, secondhand furniture, just enough love to keep the edges from cracking.

He watched without speaking. Without writing. Without claiming.

But every fall, a silent deposit arrived in the account her mother still quietly held, just enough to cover books, rent, or the Corolla's failing starter motor. No note. No sender. Just a ghost with a code.

She never asked where the money came from.

That silence became its own kind of father, not absent, exactly, but undefined. She constructed him from what wasn't there: a man-shaped space that others respected but didn't understand. There were no framed photos. No anecdotes. No heirlooms on a shelf. Just a void treated with ceremony, as if naming it might let something unwanted in.

And so, she learned to live among the unspoken.

She carried herself like someone who noticed more than she let on, but not always in the ways that mattered most. Her expression was calm, deliberate. People mistook her restraint for aloofness. In truth, she simply didn't volunteer pieces of herself, not for flattery, not for comfort. She was courteous, efficient, and emotionally precise, but trusting in places she didn't realize could be dangerous.

At work, she earned respect without ever asking for it. Her clients didn't know much about her, just that she handled complicated matters with startling clarity. Lost pensions. Legal affidavits. Paper trails gone cold. She untangled red tape without judgment or showmanship. People left her office feeling steadied.

Outside, she moved the same way, alone but never exposed. She was the kind of woman who walked home with her keys between her fingers, just in case.

She worked in a small, dim office above the Busy Bee restaurant at Damen and Milwaukee, where the scent of fried onions mixed with old varnish and commuter dust. The stairs were steep, the railing loose, and the windows rattled whenever the Blue Line screamed past. But she liked it there. It felt lived-in, like an extension of the city's pulse. It didn't pretend to be anything it wasn't.

The office was spare: one battered metal desk, a leaning coat rack, cabinets that stuck when you opened them too quickly. A mismatched chair for guests. Nothing green or soft. The walls had last been painted during the Nixon years, a dull ivory gone yellow with time.

But she made it work. She didn't decorate, didn't personalize. No photos, no knickknacks. Just paperwork, a reliable pen, and a precise stack of forms labeled with tabs so crisp they might as well have been military.

People came for help. Not flashy people, not high-powered types, but the ones who got overlooked elsewhere. The elderly, the undocumented, the recently widowed. She had a way of explaining things without making people feel stupid. They remembered that. And they came back.

She didn't talk much about herself, not at work, not with neighbors, not even with the few people who might have counted as friends. Her answers to personal questions were polite but deflective. A nod. A shrug. A glance at the time.

Dating seemed like a foreign language she once understood but never spoke fluently. If there were men in her life, they passed through quietly. No one met them. No one asked. There might have been someone once, the echo of a laugh, the way a song felt too familiar, the faint sense that she'd once been seen in a softer light. But nothing that lasted, nothing that ever took root. And she seemed fine with that. Comfortable, even.

After work, she'd walk home with a cloth bag slung over one shoulder. Usually she stopped for groceries, simple things: lentils, onions, a small container of sour cream. She avoided eye contact in line but always said thank you. She tipped in cash. If a kid behind her dropped something, she'd kneel to pick it up. Her kindness was quiet, the kind that asked for nothing in return.

It was the sort of life no one wrote songs about.

But it was hers.

And she had earned every inch of it.

She was sharp. Not just in her work, but in the way she observed the world, like she was always clocking exits, sensing people's motives before they even spoke. She wasn't paranoid, just prepared. Years of living between systems, city and state, immigrant and native, woman and worker, had taught her how quickly things could fall apart if you weren't paying attention.

Her clients noticed it too. Not just the efficiency, but the sense of calm she brought to bureaucratic chaos. A frantic widow trying to locate her husband's military pension would leave with a roadmap and a strange sense of relief. An old man struggling with Medicaid forms would be reassured before she even said a word, because she didn't treat him like a burden.

That kind of presence couldn't be taught. It was something earned through weathering small, constant storms.

People asked why she didn't go bigger. Open a firm. Run for office. Do more.

But they never understood: she was doing more.

Quietly. Precisely.

She didn't want scale, she wanted truth. And truth, she believed, lived in the small things. The overlooked details. The act of helping someone without anyone else noticing.

What she didn't know, what she could never know, was that her life had been shaped by a shadow. Not interfered with, not controlled, but watched. Gently, deliberately. From across streets. Through smeared windshields. Behind newspaper pages folded just high enough to keep her in view.

There were moments, rare ones, where she felt something. A flicker at the edge of her vision. A car she'd seen twice in the same day. A man standing at the corner, gone when she looked back. But nothing ever stuck. She'd dismiss it. Too much coffee. Not enough sleep. Just the city playing tricks.

And maybe that was for the best.

Because the truth wouldn't have comforted her.

The truth was a man who had once been erased from her story, now holding to its margins with quiet loyalty. Not to change her course. Not to ask for thanks. But simply to be near.

And in the ledger of his long, silent life, her existence was the only entry that mattered.

In a city that swallowed people whole, he had never let her be one of them.

He never reached out.

But he never let go.

Chapter 6: The Facade

It started on a Thursday.

She had just locked the office door and stepped into the gray-orange haze of early evening. The hallway behind her still smelled faintly of fried onions and copy toner. Outside, the heat hit her like a wall, the kind that makes your scalp prickle and your breath catch. The city was sweating, and it wasn't just the people. The bricks, the streetlamps, the mailboxes, everything radiated back the day's misery like a grudge.

The sidewalk shimmered faintly. Car alarms chirped without urgency. Somewhere overhead, the El screamed past in a gust of sparks and noise. Down below, a dog barked behind a fence, its hoarse voice bouncing between buildings. It was the kind of heat that turned exhaust into its own atmosphere, metallic, bitter, and endless. You could taste it if you inhaled too deep.

She adjusted her bag, pushed the office key deep into her coat pocket, and started walking toward the corner.

There were still people on the street, not many, but enough to keep you half-aware. A woman in blue scrubs walking with purpose. Two older men in white tank tops arguing in Polish, gesturing more than speaking. Kids dragging plastic skateboards behind them like forgotten limbs. Everyone moving through their own bubble, but still tangibly part of the same heavy air.

And then there was the man across the street.

He wasn't watching her. Wasn't smiling. Just leaning on a short railing outside the pawn shop, sipping something from a paper cup. One foot crossed over the other. Loose posture. Still.

She noticed him the way you notice a new pothole on your route to work, not worth swerving for, but something your mind logs and bookmarks without permission.

***

He was there again the next day.

Same time. Same paper cup. Same lean against the railing like it had been assigned to him. This time, their eyes met. He gave a nod, not inviting, not strange. Just acknowledgment. Like two people recognizing each other at a bus stop they never planned to share.

She didn't return it. But she didn't look away, either.

There was something about the way he stood that made it hard to ignore, not the man himself, but the stillness. In a city that pulsed and shifted constantly, his lack of movement was louder than any siren. No headphones. Just him and whatever he was drinking, watching the day drift past like it didn't concern him.

Three days later, she saw him again.

This time, it was during lunch. She carried her little stained Tupperware tray down the block to the bench near the old newspaper box, a forgotten patch of sidewalk that sat in the shade for half the day. She liked it. You could eat there without talking to anyone, and the traffic noise was just loud enough to drown out your own thoughts.

He was already sitting there.

One arm draped across the backrest. Same brown paper bag at his side. He glanced up and gave the same nod, easy, unfazed, like he'd been waiting for no one in particular.

She nearly walked past. But something about the way he didn't shift made her pause.

"You mind if I sit?"

He slid over without a word.

She sat down, a good two feet of polite distance between them. They didn't speak. He pulled a sandwich from the bag. She peeled the lid off a container of leftover stew. The pigeons arrived like they had a standing appointment.

***

Before she stood to leave, he spoke.

"Busy Bee's smells better than it tastes."

She looked sideways at him, not startled, but unsure if he was talking to her.

Then she gave a quiet smile. "That's fair."

He didn't follow up, didn't elaborate. Just returned his attention to the pigeons, who were now circling like critics.

The next day, same bench. He was already there.

She considered going somewhere else, there were a few concrete planters by the bank that passed for seating, but found herself walking the same route, feet making the decision before her mind could intervene.

He scooted over again. She sat again. No questions asked.

That was how it started.

They spoke, now and then, mostly about the weather, the traffic, the strange woman who shouted at light poles near the laundromat. He once asked what she did. She answered vaguely: forms, assistance, documents. He didn't pry.

She asked what he did. He said, "Repairs."

"What kind?"

He gave a shrug. "Whatever needs fixing."

He said it like a man who didn't expect admiration, or even interest, just stating fact.

One day, he brought her coffee.

Strong. Bitter. From the little shop two doors down that always used too-thin paper cups with tight-fitting lids.

"You looked tired yesterday," he said.

She hesitated, then accepted it with a nod. She didn't drink it that day, set it aside and poured it out later, but she did the next time.

There was never a declaration, never a moment where either of them defined the arrangement. It just became a rhythm. A city ritual. Two lives brushing edges, unspoken and uncommitted.

That's how it worked in places like this.

That's how most things began.

***

Weeks passed before he ever crossed the threshold.

One afternoon, she heard a soft knock, not urgent, not loud. Just enough to cut through the clatter of the office fan and the far-off screech of the El. She looked through the narrow window beside the glass door. He stood there, rain-damp and sheepish, holding a manila folder in one hand.

"Said you were a notary," he offered when she opened the door.

"I am."

He handed over the form, something simple, maybe a vehicle title or a lease. Nothing that caught her attention. She stamped it, signed it, and handed it back. He thanked her with a small nod, then left without stepping past the mat.

The next time, he brought coffee again. Said nothing about it. Just set it on the edge of her desk and left.

Then it was a package.

"Mind if this gets delivered here?" he asked. "Just once. My building's got issues."

She agreed. Then agreed again. And again.

Next came the bag of tools, old, heavy, scratched from real use. He asked to stash them under the stairwell for a night.

"Too heavy to lug around," he said. "Won't be in the way."

They weren't.

Once, he asked to use the sink. Said he'd been working all morning, nowhere nearby to wash up. He rolled up his sleeves and scrubbed his arms with focus, like a surgeon before a cut. She watched from the doorway, something about the silence between them stretching and taut.

Still, he never lingered.

Never made himself bigger than the room.

And always left without a trace, no smell, no suggestion, no pressure.

She told herself it meant nothing.

But she double-locked the door after he left, every time.

Just in case.

***

She didn't mark the moment it shifted.

There was no kiss. No confession. No flickering montage of hands brushing in the dark. Just a slow erosion of the space between them, the kind you don't notice until your coat hangs beside someone else's and your groceries are bought in twos.

One afternoon, she brought him cookies from the Polish bakery. The good kind, still warm in the wax paper bag. She offered them without ceremony. He looked at her, surprised like she'd handed him something too fragile to deserve.

"Thanks," he said. Then added, "You didn't have to."

"I know."

He sat on the bench and split one with her, silent, chewing like it meant something.

After that, there were more shared things, not gifts, not gestures. Just small collisions of routine. A coffee left by the door. A jacket loaned on a cold day. A phone call, once, when her light had stayed on too long and he'd "just wanted to check."

He never used her name. She wasn't sure if he even knew it. But when they passed each other in the stairwell or the alley, it felt like something exchanged hands, not romance, but familiarity. Not a spark, but a pilot light.

He asked her to dinner once. Just once.

Nothing fancy. A bowl of soup, some pierogi, a table tucked near the back of a café that smelled like boiled cabbage and floor cleaner.

He didn't try to charm her.

He let her talk. About the office. The busted elevator. The people she couldn't help. The man who came in every Tuesday just to ask what day it was.

He listened without nodding.

Without smiling.

But she could tell, he heard everything.

That was the most dangerous part.

***

The first time he stayed late, it wasn't planned.

The rain had come hard and sideways, blurring the alley like a wash of old film. She'd told him to wait it out — "No point in getting soaked." He stood awkwardly near the window while she made tea, dripping onto the tile like a guilty dog.

She handed him a towel. He sat on the couch, rubbing it over his head in quiet circles. When he finished, he folded it neatly on his lap and stared at his hands.

"You good?" she asked.

He looked up, blinked once, and nodded. "Yeah. Just tired."

She didn't ask from what. Didn't ask where he lived, or if he had someone waiting.

Those questions didn't feel allowed.

Instead, she sat on the other end of the couch and turned on the radio. Low volume. Just enough to fill the space between them with someone else's voice.

After that, it became a rhythm. He'd drop by on late afternoons, always with a reason. A document. A busted watch. A story about the weirdo at the pawn shop who tried to sell a blender full of coins.

She laughed more than she meant to. Not because he was funny, he wasn't, but because he knew how to leave space. To let things land.

One day, his boots were by the door.

Another, his razor was in the medicine cabinet.

She never invited him to move in.

He never asked.

But he was there.

Not like a crash.

Like a fog.

One morning, she woke to find him asleep in the chair across from her, his head tilted back, mouth open just slightly. There was a moment, silent, intimate, unearned, where she wondered what he looked like as a boy.

Then she stood up.

And made coffee.

***

They never argued. That was part of it.

She'd had relationships before, the kind with friction and sharp edges, full of long text messages and slammed doors. This was different. Quiet. Easy. Deceptively so.

He was grateful. Always. Or at least he seemed to be. A nod, a small smile, a murmured "thanks" when she handed him a sandwich or let him borrow the keys to the back stairwell.

But he never gave much back.

Not resentment. Not affection. Not plans. Just… presence.

She didn't ask for more, not at first. It felt like trespassing to even think it.

45

Still, sometimes, in the shower or during commercials or brushing her teeth at night, the questions would sneak in.

Where did he go when he left?

How did he pay for things?

He always had cash. Small bills. Folded tight. Tucked into the inner pocket of that gray canvas coat he wore, even in warm weather.

She once joked, "You stash all your money in the lining of that thing?"

He didn't laugh. Just said, "Better than banks," and changed the subject.

The signs were there, not screaming, but whispering.

The paperwork that didn't match.

The package she signed for, labeled under someone else's name.

She asked him about it, gently. Casually. "Hey, you using an alias now?"

He looked at her for half a second too long.

Then smiled. "Just a dumb inside joke."

She smiled back.

But something had shifted.

She didn't know it yet, but the slope had already begun.

It wasn't a cliff. It was a long, slow slide.

And the ground was starting to give.

***

She hadn't seen him for three days. No bench. No knock on the door. Not even the usual paper cup left in the recycling bin under the stairs, a small, dumb thing she'd grown used to noticing.

At first, she didn't mind. People had lives. Jobs. Maybe he was out of town. Maybe he'd gotten sick.

But by the fourth day, she noticed she was waiting.

She paused longer by the corner. Opened the office blinds just a little wider. Went to the bench during lunch, though it was cold and the wind was picking up.

He reappeared the next day like nothing had happened. Same nod, same half-smile.

She didn't ask.
He didn't offer.

But that was the first time she caught herself wondering if she should be worried.

Not worried for his safety.
Worried for herself, for the way the space he left behind felt *noticeable*.

That week, his stories started to get longer. A little more detailed.

He talked about a neighbor who played his TV too loud, about a tool order that got delayed, about a niece who might move in.

None of it was strange on its own. But it came all at once.

She realized he was filling silence, like someone trying to paper over a crack.

That's when she asked if he had anyone.

It came out sideways, wrapped in a joke about his niece — "So you're the family man now?"

He didn't laugh. Just shrugged. "Family's complicated."

That was the end of that line.

Later, she tried to remember why she hadn't asked more.

But that was part of it.

He never raised her suspicions.

He just redirected them, like a street you meant to take but missed without noticing.

*****

On a bench outside the Damen Blue Line station, Big Shoe sat alone, one ankle resting over the other, a newspaper spread neatly in his lap. He wasn't reading it.

His eyes, behind thick-rimmed glasses, were still.

A low wind stirred leaves against the curb as the couple emerged from the mouth of the station, the girl and the man.

They didn't see him.

She walked with her hands tucked into her coat sleeves, shoulders drawn in, talking softly. The man gestured as he spoke, animated and easy, smiling at something she said. He touched her elbow lightly as they crossed Milwaukee, then let his hand linger just a moment too long.

He didn't move.

His eyes tracked them, slow and deliberate, like tracing the path of a slow leak.

There was no menace in the man's walk, only calculation. Too fluid. Too charming. His smile was just a beat ahead of his eyes.

Big Shoe had seen it before. Dozens of versions.

Different faces. Same predator.

He turned a page of the paper without reading it, then folded it crisply down the middle.

As they vanished down the sidewalk, swallowed by the afternoon crowd, he stood, slow, heavy, and tucked the folded paper under his arm.

His expression never changed. There was no glint of recognition. No hint of emotion.

Just a final glance in their direction.

Then he turned, stepped off the curb, and disappeared into the pulse of the city.

***

Two days later, the man was back, waiting at the old bus stop outside her building with two coffees balanced on the slat beside him and a scarf draped over his knee.

She hesitated.

"Don't get weird about it," he said, holding the scarf out like it was a receipt. "I have extras."

She took it.
It smelled faintly like sawdust and cloves.

That week, they started seeing each other more at night, not always planned. One night she called out to him across the street without thinking.

He crossed over without a word and just walked beside her. No questions. No pressure.

The air between them started to feel charged, not with romance, but with something quieter. Dependency maybe.

Not the kind you admit to.

The kind that grows like mold behind the walls.

She caught herself glancing at the coat rack, looking for his jacket.

She started buying an extra coffee in the mornings, just in case he stopped by.

One Friday, he asked if she wanted to see a movie.

"Sure," she said, too fast.

"Any preferences?"

"Anything but a romance."

He grinned. "Deal."

They didn't hold hands. He didn't try to kiss her. They sat through a moody crime drama in silence, then walked home without much talking.

At her door, he paused. "You ever think about getting out of this neighborhood?"

She looked up. "You offering me an escape plan?"

He gave that half-smile again. "No. Just wondering if you have one."

She didn't answer.

Not that night.

Not yet.

Chapter 7: Setting the Hook

It began, as it always does, with small things.

He forgot his wallet one afternoon and asked to borrow twenty bucks for groceries. She hesitated, then handed it over. He paid her back the next day, just as he said he would. Then he forgot again. And again. A twenty here. A lunch there. She stopped keeping track.

Then came the packages.

Just one at first — "Mail's a mess in my building," he explained, casual and self-effacing. "Just need to have it delivered here this once." She nodded. It didn't seem like a big deal. But then came another. And another. Five. Ten. Stacked boxes waiting near the copier. She joked he was running a warehouse. He smiled and said, "Just a side hustle." Then opened one to show her. Toner cartridges. Printer ink. Boring, beige boxes full of nothing.

That was part of the trick.

He made the lie boring.

He talked about starting a business, office supply resale. Low-margin, unglamorous, but "recession-proof," he said. He had a lead on a bulk supplier. Good rates, steady demand. He even mentioned a cousin who did something similar in Indiana.

She laughed. "That's the most practical scam I've ever heard."

He didn't flinch.

"Exactly."

A week later, he mentioned needing a short-term storage unit for inventory. Just a few months, until things flipped. The problem was his credit, an old medical bill had tanked it. Would she mind co-signing?

He made it sound like joining a gym.

She hesitated. Not because she didn't trust him, but because it felt like a crossing point. Something important. Something invisible.

But he didn't beg.

Didn't push.

He just waited, quietly, like the answer was already hers and he'd accept whatever it was.

She signed.

That was the first hook.

***

After the storage unit, the rhythm returned. Coffee. Small talk. Long silences on the bench. Nothing felt different, not right away. But it was. The shift was subtle, like a rug pulled slowly, an inch at a time, under someone too distracted to notice.

A few weeks later, he mentioned the business credit card.

"Just temporary," he said, as if talking to himself. "Gets me started. I'll move it into my name once the LLC paperwork clears."

She didn't answer right away. He didn't press. That was his pattern, let her fill the space. Let her convince herself. It was never a hard sell.

The card arrived a week later.

He took a picture of it in his hand and texted her: *"Official now. Appreciate you more than you know."*

She didn't reply, but she smiled when she read it.

It was maxed out in two weeks.

He explained it away like a man who believed it. A supplier had doubled the order, mistake on their end, but no refunds until next month. Just a shipping error. Just timing. He showed her a typed invoice with a grainy logo and vague line items. It looked real enough. It was designed to.

"I'd float it myself if I could," he said. "I just didn't want to lose momentum."

She nodded, pretending to understand.

That was the thing. It all *sounded* like business. There was a logic to it, a mundane, half-boring logic. No wild promises. No pressure.

It never felt like a scam.

It felt like a man trying.

That was the second hook.

And the moment where everything began to slip, though she wouldn't realize it until much later, when her name would appear on things she didn't remember signing.

Chapter 8: Checking In

He made the call from a pay phone two blocks away, outside a shuttered laundromat with cracked windows and a broken Coke machine out front.

She picked up on the second ring. "Well?"

"She signed for the card," he said. "Didn't even need a pitch. I just sat there and let her talk herself into it."

A pause. Then laughter, light, sharp, amused. "You're such a prince."

He grinned. "Prince Charming, baby. With toner cartridges and sad eyes."

"Hook, line, and sinker?"

"Deep enough I could yank her out of the lake backwards. She thinks it's her idea — that's the real art."

She whistled. "Damn. That's your third this year."

"Fourth, technically. But this one's the cleanest. No kids. No roommates. A little lonely, a little idealistic. The kind that leaves the door unlocked if you act like you forgot your keys."

"You gonna stretch it out?"

"Couple more weeks, maybe. There's still meat on the bone."

"You're disgusting."

He chuckled. "You love it."

"I do," she said. Then quieter: "Be careful. You're getting good, but don't get sloppy."

"Always careful. She's a nice girl. Just… in the way."

The line buzzed with static for a moment. Then she said, "Call me when you've cleared the account."

He hung up without saying goodbye.

Chapter 9: The Break

Things changed after that. Not dramatically. Not all at once.

Just a fray at the edges.

He still came around. Still brought coffee sometimes. Still sat with her on the bench and talked about nothing. But he stopped listening the way he used to, not obviously, but enough that she noticed. Enough that it left a draft in the room, like someone had cracked a window.

She chalked it up to stress. The business. Money. She told herself this is what real effort looked like, distracted, tired, always managing a dozen invisible things. That's what he said, too.

"The margins are razor-thin," he told her one night as he paced the apartment. "One bad shipment, and you're bleeding."

She nodded and offered wine. He declined and went out for a smoke instead.

His eyes didn't meet hers as often. His hand on her shoulder no longer lingered. He didn't pull away, not fully. He just faded. Like something washed too many times.

Then came the payday loan.

She didn't remember authorizing it. She didn't remember signing anything at all. But her name was on the documents, signature and all. The routing number linked to her account. The dates lined up with a folder she'd helped him fill out for the LLC, back when she still thought of this as "our thing," even if she never said it out loud.

She confronted him once. Not angrily. Just confused.

He tilted his head. "You said it was okay. For the application. You even double-checked the forms."

She tried to recall. Couldn't. Maybe she had. Maybe she hadn't. It all blurred.

He looked hurt, not defensive, not guilty. Just hurt. That was the worst part.

She apologized.

That night, she woke up at 3:17 a.m. and stared at the ceiling until sunrise.

***

It all came to a head over something as dumb as pierogi and a check.

They were supposed to meet at the usual café. She arrived early, choosing the booth near the window, the one where the curtain rod always sagged in the middle. She ordered tea and waited.

He showed up fifteen minutes late, smelling like bar soap and beer. His hair was still damp, his shirt wrinkled. He slid into the booth like nothing was wrong. No apology. Just a soft "Hey."

Dinner was quiet. He asked a few vague questions about her day but didn't really listen to the answers. He picked at his food. Drank water. Didn't finish either.

She felt the silence between them like insulation. Thick. Airless.

When the check came, she reached for it automatically. He didn't stop her. She handed over her card with a practiced smile.

Declined.

She blinked, confused. Tried again.

Declined.

The waitress, young, bored, not unkind, offered a rehearsed line. "It happens more than you'd think."

He made a show of checking his jacket pocket for cash. Came up short. Looked embarrassed.

Still hoping not to make a scene, she slipped a few bills from the snap pocket of her wallet and handed them to the waitress, embarrassed, not just for him, but for what she'd let herself ignore.

Outside the café, he pulled his coat tighter. The sky had turned to ash, the wind a little sharper than it should've been.

"I've gotta take care of something," he said.

She nodded, too tired to ask. He nodded coldly and then turned and headed down the side street and disappeared into the shadows of the evening.

She walked home alone. The sound of her heels echoed longer than usual.

The apartment was quiet. Neat.

Too neat.

She dropped her bag and scanned the room. His boots weren't by the radiator. His jacket, gone. The paperback on the armrest, gone.

She opened the bathroom. No toothbrush. No razor.

She moved to the hall closet. Empty hangers swung gently like they'd been disturbed just moments earlier.

She stood in the doorway, waiting for some part of her to react. To scream. To run. To rage.

Nothing came.

In the morning, she called the credit card company from the kitchen wall phone, coiling the cord around her fingers as it rang. A woman answered, pleasant but robotic, and asked for the account number.

She gave it. Verified her name. Her mother's maiden name. Her address.

Then came the silence.

"One moment, please," the voice said.

She waited. The refrigerator clicked on behind her. A car honked faintly through the window.

The woman came back, voice unchanged. "It looks like your credit limit was increased on the 14th. Then again on the 17th. Both requests were approved."

"I didn't—" she stopped. "How much?"

"The limit was raised to ten thousand."

She gripped the phone tighter. "And the balance?"

"Currently at $9,987.22."

A pause.

"Can you tell me what it was spent on?"

More clicking. More silence.

"Several retail purchases — Sears, Highland Appliance, a wire transfer to a business account. Also three cash advances totaling three thousand."

The woman rattled it off like a recipe.

She closed her eyes. "Can you send me a copy of the full statement?"

"It'll go out in today's mail."

She thanked her. Hung up.

Then stood there for a long time with the receiver still in her hand, the dial tone humming in her ear.

Ten thousand.
It rang in her skull like a slow bell.

She set the phone down gently. Sat at the table. Pulled her robe tighter around her and stared at the sugar jar.

As the shock became tolerable, she dressed quickly, slacks, a sweater, no makeup, and walked to the nearest branch of her bank. No appointments. No calls. Just the blunt force of impulse, moving her feet forward.

The teller was young, polite, and visibly uncomfortable. She typed something, frowned, then printed the account summary. Without a word, she slid it across the counter.

Her heart skipped as she read it.

The account had been emptied over three days: Cash withdrawals in exact increments.
A money order.
Two bounced checks.

The remaining balance was 73 cents.

There was no error. No misunderstanding. No digital glitch to blame.

Just numbers. And absence.

She nodded once, muttered "Thanks," and walked out into the cold. The sun was too bright. The street noise too sharp. Her keys felt foreign in her hand.

Somewhere deep inside, a small voice whispered: You let him in.

You let this happen.

But it wasn't accusation.

It was resignation.

She walked home in the cold, coat unbuttoned, hair undone, the city noise dull behind her ears.

Chapter 10: The Celebration

The place was nearly empty. Just him and two other guys down at the end of the bar, low murmurs passing between them like tired cards in a worn deck.

He sat hunched over, nursing the tail end of a grin that hadn't fully left his face all day. One elbow on the bar, eyes tracing the swirl of scuffed varnish, basking in the quiet afterglow of a clean ripoff.

The bartender, pudgy, wiry-haired, wearing a faded Sox tee, came over, wiping his hands on a towel stiff with old beer foam.

"You want your usual Old Style?"

The scammer blinked out of his thoughts, slow to answer. Then he gave a little shake of the head.

"I'll have a Heineken."

The bartender raised an eyebrow but didn't say anything. He reached into the cooler and slid the green bottle across. The scammer didn't even look up, just popped the cap on the edge of the bar like he owned the place and took a sip.

At the other end, one of the guys laughed, a thick, wet laugh, and muttered something loud enough to catch the room. Something with a hard f-word in it.

The bartender tensed and quicky walked over.

"Hey. This is a respectable place of business. My business. I don't want to hear that kind of language in here, got it?."

Both men paused with a confused look on their face.

"Are you fuckin' kidding me?" the bigger one said. "This is a shithole bar in Cicero filled with bust outs." You think you're runnin' the Ritz here?"

He stood up slowly.
"You better back off before I jump over the bar and beat the fuck out of you, you piece of shit..."

The bartender held his ground for a heartbeat, then deflated, mumbled something, and shuffled back toward the register.

The two men drained the rest of their drinks, slapped a few bills down without counting, and headed for the door. One of them paused just long enough to shoot a final look at the bartender, not rage, not threat, just utter contempt, then pushed through the squeaking door and vanished into the night.

The scammer barely noticed. He took another sip of his Heineken, savoring the quiet. Then he stood up, walked over to the payphone near the entrance. He stepped into the nook and dropped in a quarter. The dial tone buzzed like a fly in a jar. He punched the number from memory.

His girlfriend picked up on the second ring. "Yeah?"

"It's done," he said, grinning. "Completely wiped."

She laughed, the low, throaty kind that came with menthols and bar light living.

"Didn't doubt it. Our little dumpling finally cracked?"

He held the receiver crooked between shoulder and ear.

"She signed everything. Credit's fried, savings are gone."

"Jesus. That poor bitch."

He chuckled. "I told you."

"Come home soon," she said. "I'm in the mood to celebrate."

He exhaled a thin stream of smoke, watching it curl above the receiver.

"Be there in an hour," he said. "Don't eat without me."

He hung up, let the cigarette burn between his fingers, and walked back to the bar with the hint of a smile lingering on his face.

The bartender didn't speak, just gave him a long glance before turning away to polish the same glass for the third time. The place had thinned out even more. A single neon beer sign buzzed in the window, throwing the scammer's shadow in jagged lines across the linoleum.

The Heineken was half-warm now. He didn't care.

He sat contently. Like a man who'd managed to talk his way off a sinking ship and into someone else's life raft.

He reached into his coat pocket and pulled out a slip of paper. Her handwriting, curled, polite, hopeful. A grocery list. Eggs. Rice. Garlic powder. Things they'd run out of. He stared at it, then folded it once, twice, and lit the corner. Watched the flame consume it to ash in the tray.

It wasn't guilt. Just clean up.

Chapter 11: Volání (The Call)

The small apartment smelled of dill and boiled potatoes, the air thick with a quiet grief that never fully left. Lace curtains hung heavy with age, filtering the fading evening light into narrow golden bands across the linoleum. A cuckoo clock ticked from the wall, slow and deliberate, like it was keeping time for someone else entirely.

She sat at the kitchen table, her hands folded loosely in front of her. The teacup to her right had gone cold, untouched since steeping. A plate of uneaten rye bread sat beside it, one corner torn but never lifted to her mouth. She had tried to eat earlier, out of routine more than hunger, but the thought wouldn't let her.

Across from her, near the old rotary phone on the counter, was a small photo in a plastic frame. A man, tall and unsmiling. The image was faded, but the eyes were still sharp. She stared at it now, unmoving.

She had not spoken to him in years. Not out of bitterness, but out of agreement. When she came to America, she asked for peace. Distance. And he, to his credit, had kept that promise. No visits. No phone calls. No interference.

But now things had changed.

Their daughter had come by last week. She didn't say much. Just sat at the table and cried quietly, hands folded, shoulders hunched. She said the man she was seeing had disappeared. That her savings were gone.

That she was ashamed. Not of him, but of herself. That was the part that stayed. Like a thorn beneath the skin.

The mother reached for the phone but stopped halfway. She drew the hand back and smoothed her skirt instead, fingers trembling slightly.

In the drawer by the stove, beneath the old gas bills and appliance warranties, was a piece of paper. It had not been touched in years. She slid it out carefully, unfolding it like parchment from another life. The number was still there. Faint pencil, nearly rubbed smooth.

She picked up the phone and dialed slowly. One ring. Two. Then a click. Silence. Then breath.

She did not ask if it was him. She did not say her name.

"Our daughter has been hurt," she said, her voice firm but quiet. "Not with fists. But in ways that take longer to heal."

There was no reply. Just silence. But she knew he was listening.

"She trusted someone. He took her money. But worse, he made her feel small. He made her doubt herself. You understand?"

Still nothing on the line. Just the faint sound of breathing.

"I thought you should know. Do what you will with that."

She hung up before he could respond. The click of the receiver echoed through the kitchen like a final period.

The cuckoo clock struck six. The bird emerged and chirped, then slipped away again. She returned to her chair and folded her hands, staring down at the table, the photo, the teacup now cold as stone.

The line went silent, the weight of her words still hanging there, unspent. Somewhere, the faint hum of the connection traveled out of her kitchen, across wires and switchboards, carrying the ghost of her voice into another building. It arrived in a room with no smell of tea, no warmth at all.

His room felt refrigerated, not from cold but from absence. The walls were painted a pale aquamarine, the kind of color that might've once been chosen for calm, now faded and institutional, laid thick over coarse cinderblock. It caught the light like hospital tile, soft but unfeeling.

The furnishings were spare, squared off, and dull with age, not broken, just dispassionate. A table of dull gray laminate sat beneath a low, frosted ceiling fixture, its light diffused, sterile. Only one chair. No second setting. No invitation for company.

The table was set with silent deliberation. A white plate, blank and centered. Fork and knife aligned atop a napkin folded into a perfect square, creased like it had been pressed under glass. Across from it sat a squat tabletop radio, old, Soviet-looking, with a chrome tuning dial turned halfway between stations. The low static whispered into the room like wind slipping through a crack.

No television. No photos. No ashtray. The air smelled faintly of metal and boiled coffee, like an office left behind.

Big Shoe didn't move. He sat upright at the table, the phone still pressed to his ear, as if the woman's voice might return.

But the line had gone quiet.

He listened anyway. His fingers didn't twitch. His face betrayed nothing. His lone eye, the good one, stared forward, locked in that vast, unreadable way he had. The foggy one stayed fixed, dull as clouded glass.

Then, a mechanical click. The severed line.

He held the receiver there another second, maybe two. Then lowered it gently into its cradle. The sound of the handset settling into place landed with finality. It echoed softly in the room, but nothing else moved.

He sat like that a while longer.

As if something had just arrived, not in the call, but in the silence that followed.

A full minute passed, maybe more. Then he stood.

His movements were deliberate. He crossed the room and opened a drawer built into the kitchen cabinets. Inside, laid beneath a folded dish towel, was a single photograph. He slid it out carefully and held it in both hands. It was old, the color faded, the edges softened with time. His daughter, no more than six, sat on a park bench with a paper cone of sunflower seeds in her lap. Her shoes were scuffed, but she was smiling. A genuine, unguarded smile. The kind he hadn't seen in decades.

He ran his thumb slowly across the photo, over her face, again and again. The room was quiet but for the slow ticking of a wall clock and the faint hum of radio static between stations. After a while, he placed the photo back exactly where it had been, refolded the towel, and closed the drawer.

He walked to the window.

The pastel beige curtain barely stirred as he parted it with two fingers. Outside, the street was dim, a yellowed hush hanging over the parked cars and cracked pavement. He stared down at nothing in particular, not a single expression on his face, just the stillness of a man watching the world for signs it would justify what must now be done.

Chapter 12: First Visitation (The Substation)

Near the corner of 22nd and Laramie.

The building didn't look like anything. That's what made it perfect.

Just past the alley cutout beside the plumbing supply shop, tucked into the teeth of a block-long row of tired retail carcasses, the old substation sat squat and low, its concrete face scorched dull gray by decades of sun, soot, and indifference. The city had once used it for switching power loads; now it was a dead node. Still wired, but no longer useful, like a nerve ending that remembered pain but had nothing left to feel.

Rusted bars on the only window. Inside, the air was warmer than the street. It hummed with a dry, electric fatigue. Old fluorescent tubes flickered with lazy pulses overhead, struggling to light a space that had no real desire to be seen.

The man inside called it his office, though it was really just a cinderblock room with warped vinyl tile, a metal desk, and a blinking phone he had been way from for weeks. He worked alone. Worked, meaning grifted. Letterhead scams, refund chases, stolen coupon booklets he flipped to desperate shop owners with promises of tax breaks. The sort of hustle that made money just slow enough to avoid attention.

A blue oscillating fan rattled from the filing cabinet. A plastic ashtray overflowed with cigarette butts the color of old tea bags. He was mid-call, feet up, recounting some imaginary business write-off to a maybe-client, when the hum of the fan seemed to fade, not stop, just recede, as his hearing tuned to something else.

Then the clunk.

Not a knock. Not a footstep. A *clunk*, irregular, wrong-footed. Metal on concrete. Once. Then again. Closer.

The front door was propped open with a length of cracked broom handle. Summer in Cicero made men lazy, and he liked the street breeze in the morning, liked hearing cars drift by. He craned his neck toward the sound, cupping the receiver. Just the street.

He muttered into the phone: "Hang on, someone's here."

What he meant was: *I don't like this.*

***

The shape filled the doorway.

Not suddenly. He'd been walking up the sidewalk a while, just not *noticed*. But now he was there. Standing inside the frame like a cracked hinge in human form. Tall. Crooked at the shoulders. One shoulder higher than the other, always. As if something had settled wrong years ago and no one had dared to fix it.

He wore a suit the color of dried tobacco, pressed, preserved, and two decades behind. The lapels were wide, the cut stiff, unmistakably Eastern Bloc. His tie, modest and centered, bore a faded geometric print last fashionable in 1963 Prague. His shirt was crisp at the cuffs but yellowed slightly at the seams, the kind of slow aging that suggested careful laundering in cheap soap. His glasses were thick-rimmed, dark, and squared, more function than style. Both lenses were clear, but behind the left, his eye was a white cloud, fogged over by time or trauma. The other eye, dark and sharp, did all the watching.

The man at the desk froze.

The figure stepped forward. The sound came again, not just a clunk, but a pattern. Right foot… soft. Left foot… a heavy, dead thud. Not metal. Not a brace. A shoe, too tall, too wrong. A platform lift, nearly four inches thick, built not for fashion but for function. Orthopedic. Medical. The man's left leg was shorter, and the compensating shoe gave him a lopsided gait that defied rhythm. He didn't limp, he listed. His body leaned oddly with each step, like gravity pulled him at strange angles. His arms, stiff at his sides, swung slightly out of sync, adding to the visual dissonance. Watching him walk made people uneasy, not because of pity, but because something about the motion felt *off*. Like a marionette operated by an indifferent or maybe vengeful hand. The erratic gait continued…*off-tempo*. Unsettling to watch.

In his right hand: a fork.

Not a dinner fork. Not plastic. This was steel. Three thick prongs, gleaming under the overheads.

Polished with faint residual staining that caught the light.

He raised it gently. As if showing something he'd found on the sidewalk. His voice came low, calm, accent thick but indistinct.

"I found this outside. Is it yours?"

The man didn't get a chance to move.

"Not mine," he stammered. "This ain't a soup kitchen." A weak, nervous laugh slipped out before he could stop it.

Big Shoe stepped closer, casting a heavy shadow over the desk. His voice was soft but serrated.

"You are not listening to me," he said. "I am no longer asking — I am telling you... this belongs to you."

He held the fork out, its tines reflecting the overhead lights.

The man's eyes jittered, scanning for exits, options, tools, gods.

Silence.

Three seconds passed. Each one dragged across his nerves like a razor.

Then it came, swift and surgical.

Big Shoe plunged the fork deep into the socket of his shoulder joint. The man shrieked as the metal bit bone. His chair slammed back and collapsed.

Big Shoe's left hand was already there, palm clamped over the man's mouth, muffling the howl.

The right hand twisted.

Twisted harder.

A sickening, wet pop snapped through the room. The joint separated like pulled poultry. The man's body spasmed, then one arm went limp, flopping uselessly beside him.

He writhed, one hand cradling his now-ruined shoulder.

Big Shoe leaned in, smiling faintly. His breath smelled of nothing. His face was inches away.

"Yes, my boy," he whispered. "Yes. This is the beginning of a lifetime of retribution."

The man whimpered.

"Get familiar with pain."

The man tried to scream again, but the hand stayed firm.

Tears spilled now, not just from pain but terror. His good arm clawed at Big Shoe's wrist. His eyes begged, pleaded. His legs kicked weakly against the tile.

Big Shoe tilted his head slightly, studying him. Not with anger, with the impassive curiosity of a man checking for rot in a piece of fruit.

"Be a man," he said quietly. "Stop your sniveling. Or I'll kill you now."

He let that settle. The sobs cut short, caught in the throat.

Then, smoothly, Big Shoe withdrew the fork.

A faint suction sound. The tines left a slow trickle down the neck and into the shirt collar. The man writhed, gasping, clutching his ruined arm.

Big Shoe straightened. Composed. He stepped back and looked down at the pathetic shape shivering on the floor, the body now half-curled around its own pain like a crushed insect.

He took in the desk: a half-eaten sandwich in deli paper. A paper bag slumped beside it.

Without a word, he plucked the napkin from beneath the sandwich, unfolded it, and calmly began wiping the fork. One stroke. Two. He checked the tines. Folded the napkin. Tossed it neatly into the wastebasket.

The whole thing took less than ten seconds.

Then he walked to the door. No glance back. Just the soft heel, the heavy clunk.

Right foot. Left foot. Right. Clunk.

The door creaked open.

The heat and murk of summer rushed back in from 22nd Street.

Big Shoe stepped into the light, as if he had just returned a borrowed library book. He turned left, his gait tilting the silhouette. The shoe struck the pavement like punctuation.

Clunk. Clunk.

He vanished down the sidewalk, swallowed into Cicero's summer haze.

Chapter 13: The Hospital

The light above his bed buzzed faintly, its white hum sinking into his skull like a second heartbeat. Somewhere past the drawn curtain, a nurse's shoes whispered against the vinyl floor, too soft to track but constant enough to remind him he was not alone. Or maybe not awake. He wasn't sure.

The ceiling was tiled in a grid of off-white squares, one slightly darker than the others, like a rotted tooth in a too-perfect smile. He stared at it. He didn't blink. Couldn't. Something about the drugs. Something about the pain, which came in strange delayed waves, not sharp, not searing, but low and spreading, like an ache beneath the ache.

Behind the curtain, two voices. Male. Calm. Familiar with damage.

"You see this dislocation?"

"Jesus. Yeah. I thought it was a lateral disclo—wait. Look at the anterior band."

"Right. And the glenoid rim here... it's shredded."

"Clean. Not a tear. More like… peeled."

"He had to lever under the acromion. From the angle, maybe even from behind the coracoid. That's not brute force. That's... technique."

Papers shifted. Gloves snapped. A pen clicked, once.

"Who did this to him?"

"He won't say."

"Well, they weren't improvising. Whoever it was knew

the exact depth. Look here—joint capsule's ruptured, but the deltoid's still intact. He meant to maim, not disable."

"Like orthopedic surgery, reversed."

Silence for a beat.

"You could put a dozen sports surgeons in a room with a fresh cadaver and not one of them could do this by hand. Not this fast. Not this clean."

"Not without training. Or… practice."

The curtain moved slightly. Not drawn. Not opened. Just a ripple.

The scammer swallowed. Hard. The sound was loud in his throat, like gravel sliding.

"He's conscious," one of them said, quiet now. "Pretending not to be. Let's give him a minute."

Footsteps retreated. The whisper-shoes again. Fading.

He turned his head one inch. Pain bloomed. His vision blinked out, then back.

On the tray beside his bed, a plastic cup of water. A folded towel. His shoulder was bound in a sling so tight it felt like his ribs were being taught to behave.

He closed his eyes. Not to sleep. Just to hide behind them. He had heard enough.

***

The hospital room was sterile and clean.

A muted TV in the upper corner flickered with an afternoon cooking show. The sound was off, but you could see the chef's mouth moving like a fish, smiling as he plated something soft and butter-colored. The scammer lay still beneath thin blankets, shoulder bandaged, arm immobile, his left side stiffened with pain and gauze. His face was pale and blotchy, and sweat lined the hollows under his eyes.

A corded hospital phone sat beside him on the tray. He stared at it for a long time. Then reached out, slow and deliberate, with his right hand, the good one. He picked up the receiver and dialed.

It rang twice.

"Hello?"

Her voice was the same, a little sharp at the edges, always slightly hurried. It irritated him sometimes. Right now, it felt like water down the throat.

"It's me," he said, keeping his voice low, flat. "I'm okay."

A pause. Then—

"Jesus, where the hell have you—"

"Listen. I can't talk long."

"What happened? You said—"

"I said I'm okay." He glanced at the door. "I'm in the hospital. Something happened. I'll explain later."

"Hospital? Are you—"

"I just wanted you to know I'm alright." He shifted, wincing as the pain blossomed up his shoulder. "Don't come here. Not yet."

"Why not?"

"It's complicated. I can't explain now. I will. But not over the phone." He inhaled slowly. "This isn't random."

She said nothing.

"This… this was something else. I'll tell you everything when I'm out. Just don't visit. Not yet."

"You sure?"

"Yes." His voice had weight now. Measured. "I'll call when I'm being discharged. You can pick me up then."

Another pause. Then: "Alright."

"Okay." He let it hang for a second. "Thanks."

He hung up.

The phone clicked back into the cradle.

Silence returned, broken only by the quiet whir of machines and the fluorescent buzz overhead. Outside the window, a weak sun spread across a flat rooftop. A pigeon picked at something unidentifiable near a rusted vent.

The door creaked.

A doctor stepped in. Late forties, narrow frame, thinning black hair. He wore tired eyes and a badge that didn't quite hang straight. He flipped through a chart as he walked, not bothering to sit.

"Well," he said, eyes scanning the paper. "I have to say… you're a lucky man."

The scammer gave a soft snort. "Yeah. Feels like it."

"I mean it. We see a lot of dislocations, fractures, even tears — but this…" He lowered the chart slightly and looked at him. "Whoever did this? They knew what they were doing."

A small bead of sweat rolled down the patient's temple. He didn't answer.

"The angle, the depth… the way the joint was separated without fracturing the clavicle or humerus? That takes knowledge. Serious anatomical knowledge. We had three surgeons in there, and every one of them said the same thing — they've never seen something this precisely devastating."

He closed the folder with a soft thump. "You're damn lucky you didn't lose the arm."

The scammer blinked slowly, then gave a weak, lopsided smile. "Great. Thanks, Doc."

The doctor paused at the foot of the bed. "Police will probably want to talk to you when you're up to it."

He shrugged, or tried to. "Yeah. Sure."

"Well." The doctor gave a little nod. "Rest up. We'll keep the pain under control. PT will be in tomorrow to assess movement."

He left.

The door clicked softly shut.

The scammer exhaled and turned his head toward the remote. It was just out of reach. He stretched with his good arm, grabbed it, and pointed it at the TV. The cooking show had been replaced by a talk show. Some puffed-up host was laughing too loudly at his own joke. The camera panned to a woman with high cheekbones.

Mute.

He turned the volume up two clicks, then back down. Then he clicked through three channels and landed on a local news update. Police were investigating a string of credit card skimming incidents on the South Side. He didn't care.

He clicked again. A show about animals. Then another with old black-and-white movies. Finally, he clicked it off.

Silence returned.

He lay still for a while. Then picked up the call button and pressed it once.

A minute passed.

A nurse's voice crackled through the intercom. "Yes?"

"Do you have any morphine?" he asked, without inflection.

A pause.

"I'll let the doctor know you're in pain."

He dropped the call button back on the bed and closed his eyes.

The fluorescent lights hummed above, indifferent.

Outside, the sun shifted slightly, crawling along the rooftop vents.

***

He sat slumped in the molded plastic chair near the nurse's station, his left arm braced in a sling, his right leg twitching with impatience. The hospital hallway smelled like vinegar and bandages, and the floor tiles had the sheen of something recently mopped but never truly clean. His name was called flatly, no warmth, no inflection, by a woman with a clipboard and a mole shaped like a comma under her eye.

"Mr. Lapinski?" she said, glancing up only once.

He stood slowly, favoring his good side, teeth clenched as he adjusted to the sharp pull in his shoulder.

"Follow me."

He did.

The discharge room had no windows. Just a pale blue wall, a laminated chart about opioid side effects, and a broken clock stuck at 3:17. She handed him a folder thick with instructions, warnings, and a prescription for painkillers that wouldn't be enough.

"You'll want to avoid lifting anything heavier than a coffee cup for the next six weeks," she said, tapping the paperwork. "Ice and elevation. Physical therapy referral's in there. Follow up in ten days."

He didn't respond. Just nodded once, jaw tight.

She slid a pen across the desk for him to sign. He scrawled something that resembled his name.

"Do you have a ride?"

"Yeah," he said. "She's on her way."

The nurse stared at him a moment longer than necessary. Her eyes dropped to the sling, the bandages, then back up to his face.

"Well... you're lucky. That kind of joint damage, you could've been saying goodbye to the arm."

He gave a forced laugh, dry and shallow. "Yeah. Real professional job."

The nurse didn't smile.

He sat alone after she left, eyes on the scuffed tile. He could still hear the words from two nights ago, muffled under that gloved hand: *Get familiar with pain.* They had followed him into his dreams, echoing through morphine fog.

Now the fog had thinned. The pain was still there, dull and mean. But he was thinking clearly again. Clear enough to know he needed to control the narrative.

He picked up the envelope of discharge papers, tucked it under his arm, and walked slowly to the lobby. The sliding glass doors yawned open to an overcast sky and the stink of summer pavement.

Her car wasn't there yet. Good. Gave him time to rehearse the lie one more time.

He lit a cigarette with shaky fingers. The nicotine barely touched the edge of it. He took two drags, then flicked it into the hospital landscaping just as the tan Corolla pulled up to the curb. She leaned across the seat, popped the door without a word.

He slid into the passenger seat, careful not to jar his shoulder. The sling itched. The stitches pulled. But he kept his face flat.

"Hey," she said, without looking at him.

"Drive," he said.

She didn't ask where. She knew the drill. They pulled out onto the main road, the world sliding past in smeared streaks of beige and gray. For a few minutes, the car was silent but for the hum of tires and the metronome click of the turn signal she forgot to cancel.

"Where to?" she finally asked.

He pointed with his chin. "That old gravel lot behind the bowling alley. Nobody goes there."

She made a turn without a word.

He didn't speak until they parked, and even then, it took him another minute. He stared out the windshield at a torn mattress someone had dumped in the weeds. A red lighter lay half-buried in gravel. A seagull hopped across the roof of a nearby warehouse like it was looking for something it had lost.

Then he exhaled.

"It wasn't random," he said.

She glanced over.

"I mean the guy — the one who did this. It wasn't just some mugger or tweaker. This was something else."

She frowned. "You said it was a robbery."

"I did. And I was lying." His tone was flat, almost bored. "He didn't take a thing. Didn't even check my pockets."

"So what was it?"

"I think it was a warning."

"From who?"

He shook his head slowly. "Don't know yet. But the guy... he was old-school. Real old-school. Like... Soviet bloc. Military precision. And the way he moved, the way he used that fork—"

"Fork?"

"Yeah. A goddamn meat fork. Did more damage than a power drill. Doctor said it looked like a surgical procedure."

She blinked.

He turned to her finally, eyes sharp.

"This is bigger than we thought."

She bit her lower lip, chewing on the thought. "You think it's connected to... her?"

"I don't know yet?"

She nodded.

He reached over with his good hand, tapped her thigh lightly.

"We'll get out of town for a while," he said, eyes still forward. "Not too far. Just enough to let things cool off."

She didn't respond, just adjusted her grip on the wheel.

"It'll blow over," he added. "It always does."

Chapter 14: Laying Low (The Hotel, Rockford)

The motel had no name you'd remember, just a battered blue sign with half its letters missing. Maybe it once said something, *Prairie View* or *Budget Lodge*, but by now it only read **IN__O_** in flickering tubes that buzzed louder than the cicadas. It squatted low along a forgotten stretch of road just off the Rockford bypass, its parking lot chewed up by years of thaw and neglect. The white paint had peeled to a dull gray, and a sagging ice machine outside the office looked like it hadn't dispensed a cube since the Carter administration.

No one stayed here for a good reason. You came if you had no better option. If you were running from someone, or something, or maybe just yourself. If you paid in cash and didn't mind stains. If you needed quiet, not the peaceful kind, but the kind no one dares to interrupt.

The building stretched in an L-shape around the lot, twenty rooms across, ten along the side wing. All single-story. No lobby, no breakfast, just a narrow office with thick Plexiglas and a small dusty TV playing reruns of *Divorce Court* on mute. The night clerk was a broad-shouldered man in a mechanic's jacket who rarely stood. Most guests never saw him upright. He just slid room keys across the counter like he was dealing bad hands of poker, barely glancing up.

Room numbers were painted on crooked plastic plaques bolted to the doors. Half were upside-down or missing digits entirely. Room 104 had its numbers drawn on in Sharpie. Room 117 had no number at all, just a faint ghost of adhesive where one had been. Nobody asked questions. If the plumbing worked, and the door locked from the inside, you were ahead of the game.

At night, the lot turned into a mirror. Shallow puddles formed over cracked asphalt, reflecting whatever little light remained, neon signs, weak porch bulbs, the occasional sputter of a passing car's taillights. Oil slicks moved slowly in the water like bruises in motion. The motel's silence wasn't the kind that felt safe. It was the kind that knew better than to get involved.

Some nights, the air carried voices: muffled arguments, low TV chatter, the strained gasps of sex through thin drywall. But mostly, it was the hum of the vending machine, the crackle of insects frying against bug zappers, and the mechanical wheeze of aging air conditioners pushing out warm air that smelled faintly of mold and burnt copper.

At the edge of the lot, weeds pushed through the concrete in slow defiance. A wooden fence, long since collapsed in places, failed to separate the property from the brush behind it. Somewhere in that overgrowth, a busted shopping cart lay on its side, half-swallowed by tall grass and time.

The second-to-last unit on the main wing, Room 109, had its curtain perpetually drawn shut. The slats were bent inward near the center, just wide enough for someone inside to peek out. That curtain never moved. It hadn't in days.

The motel's clientele came and went without names. A man with a cane. A woman with green hair who always wore sunglasses at night. A couple who checked in with no luggage and hadn't left the room in nearly a week. No one made eye contact. Everyone paid in advance.

The only rule posted anywhere was a hand-written sign in the front office:

NO REFUNDS.

It was taped up beside a candy bar rack with nothing but off-brand gum and melted peanut clusters.

During the day, the place looked almost abandoned. Paint curling off stucco. Rust bleeding from the gutters. Cigarette butts forming constellations on the stairs. But at night, in the rain, it took on a strange kind of life, wet and quiet and indifferent. A place waiting for something to happen but never quite surprised when it does.

The cops didn't come out here. Not unless someone bled loud enough. And even then, they came slow.

There was no security camera. Just a fake black dome bolted above the office door, blinking red like it was recording. It wasn't.

A place like this had no memory. Just residue. Stains that wouldn't wash out and dents that didn't matter. It didn't care who you were or why you came. It only asked one thing: cash up front and don't ask for a second key.

And that's why Room 109 was perfect.

***

Inside Room 109, the walls were the color of wet cardboard. The kind of beige that couldn't be named, just a muted sickness painted over and over to hide things that wouldn't stay hidden. One wall bore a stain the shape of Texas. Another had a patch of mismatched spackle where someone had once punched clean through. The carpet was damp near the bathroom and always smelled faintly of vinegar, no matter how many times they sprayed the travel-size Febreze they bought at the gas station.

The man sat at the room's single table, rolling a cigarette between his fingers. He didn't smoke it. Just rolled it back and forth like it was a dice that never got thrown. Across from him, the woman lay on the bed, legs tangled in the stiff comforter, one foot tapping absently as she read a gossip magazine that was three months out of date.

"You're wearing the same hoodie again," he said without looking up.

"So?"

He shrugged. "Just saying."

92

She didn't answer. Just turned a page and let it wrinkle. Her fingernail clicked against a half-empty bottle of nail polish on the nightstand. The label was peeled off. Everything in the room had its label peeled off.

He got up and walked to the window, parted the blinds with two fingers, and peeked out.

"You're gonna wear a groove in those blinds."

"They're already grooved."

"Well, try not to leave your name in it."

She flipped another page. The magazine was mostly perfume ads and diet pill promises, the kind that whispered directly to women like her: tired, uncertain, on the run from something they couldn't name.

Outside, the parking lot glistened under the weak light of a busted lamppost. The same green pickup was still parked sideways near the vending machine, hood up like it was mid-yawn.

"I'm just saying," he said finally, stepping away from the window. "We've been here a while."

She let out a small laugh. "Six nights isn't *a while*."

"It is when you're waiting for the other shoe to drop."

"You mean *his* shoe?"

He didn't answer.

Instead, he grabbed the vodka from the counter, a cheap plastic bottle with a cracked cap, and took a long pull. Then he poured some into one of the motel's cloudy plastic cups and held it out to her. She sat up and took it, drinking without expression.

"I dreamed about him again," she said, almost casually.

"Don't start."

"I'm just saying."

"You *always* just say."

She laid back, head against the cold wall, and closed her eyes. Her voice went flat. "He was behind the curtain. Just standing there."

"Jesus."

"He wasn't doing anything. Just waiting."

He looked at her. "You need to stop thinking like that."

"You think that matters?"

He didn't answer right away. The radio on the nightstand was turned down low, a hum of static between late-night ballads. Something about love gone wrong in Memphis. He sat down on the edge of the bed and stared at the floor.

"I keep telling you," he said. "He's not gonna find us."

She turned and looked at him, eyes narrowed.

"You're slipping," she said. "You left the bathroom light on all night. You tossed the ice bucket on the floor and never picked it up. You haven't shaved in four days."

He got up abruptly and moved to the kitchenette. Poured another drink. Then another.

"I'm tired, alright?" he said. "I'm tired of looking over my shoulder. I'm tired of the same goddamn questions. And I'm tired of sleeping next to someone

94

who keeps telling me I'm slipping while she watches *me* for the signs."

She stared at him a long time, then stood up. Slid the hoodie off and dropped it on the chair. Her voice was quiet.

"Then stop looking over your shoulder. Look here."

He didn't say anything.

She stepped toward him, slow, barefoot, the linoleum cool under her feet. The vodka burned between them like a wick.

"Forget him for one night."

He looked up at her, the muscles in his jaw clenched tight, his hands still around the plastic cup like he wanted to crush it.

After a moment, he set it down.

They moved toward the bed together, awkward at first, like people trying to remember how they used to be. They didn't kiss. They didn't undress slowly. Just a wordless shuffle of limbs and clothes and friction under a too-thin blanket. The mattress squeaked like a complaint, then went still.

Outside, the rain ticked steadily on the windowpane.

Inside, the radio kept humming. The song changed. The voices stayed the same.

***

Outside the rain had thinned to a steady drizzle, a whispering sort of fall that slicked the asphalt into mirror and shadow. The parking lot, long and uneven, reflected the motel's fractured light in broken smears, one bulb fully dead, another flickering, and a third buzzing like it had something to say but no one to say it to.

Toward the far end, a woman screamed, not in panic, but argument. Her voice cracked, tired and shrill, bouncing off the motel wall as she slapped the side of a beat-up Ford and called the man inside it something that didn't require a rebuttal. He lit a cigarette and stared through her like fog. The motel didn't care. Neither did anyone else.

Past them, past the soft halo of weak porch lights, beyond the buzz of the vending machine that hadn't worked in years, something moved.

A man. But not just any man.

He moved with precision that made him seem *measured*, not slow, like each step had already been rehearsed, filed away, and pulled up now from memory. He wore an outdated poor fitting trench coat that didn't quite match the decade. His head was tilted down slightly, not from age or exhaustion, but from discipline, like he walked that way always. Eyes fixed at mid-chest height. Not looking for anything. Looking *at* everything.

The puddles in his path didn't ripple when he stepped near. They only trembled after he'd passed.

He stopped beside a parked car, pale yellow, weatherworn, the shape unmistakable even in the dark: a Volkswagen Beetle. Late sixties, maybe early seventies. One hubcap missing. Rust clustering in tight constellations around the wheel wells. A frayed pair of dice dangled from the rearview mirror, stiff with age, unmoving.

He placed one hand gently on the hood.

Not a pat. Not an inspection. A glide, slow and reverent, like the first stroke across cold skin. His palm moved in a deliberate line across the wet metal, fingers parting rivulets of rain, dragging the moisture like threads across a surface that hadn't felt attention in years. He moved with the touch of someone reacquainting himself with something intimate, something that once responded.

His hand swept along the fender, over the domed trunk lid, pausing just above the emblem. There, his fingers hovered for a moment, barely grazing it, as if waiting to see whether it would resist. He didn't blink. Didn't breathe. Then his fingertips pressed down.

The curve of the VW badge gave slightly under his touch, just enough. He let his hand settle there. Not grasping it yet. Just *resting* on it, like one might place a hand on the bare back of a sleeping lover. His head tilted slightly. Not curiosity, approval. A private nod to a silent memory.

Then, slowly, he leaned in.

Rain traced quiet lines down his coat, off the brim of his hat, dripping onto the chrome with a sound too soft to matter. The air between him and the car seemed to thicken, close in, hold still.

That's when the corner of his lip moved.

Just a little. Almost imperceptible.

Not a grin. Not joy.

A smile drawn from some place deeper, mechanical, mirthless, memorized. Something that lived only in the small muscles of the face and nowhere near the heart. The moonlight caught the angle of his cheek, glinted faintly, and then, there it was: the briefest flash as the light bounced from his silver tooth.

From his coat pocket he produced a multitool, old, maybe military surplus. Worn in a way that suggested long use and careful maintenance. The kind of object that lives in a drawer until it's needed for something serious.

He unfolded it without looking. The pliers gleamed briefly in the neon wash of the motel's dying vacancy sign. He slipped them beneath the edge of the VW's badge, that circle enclosing the stacked "V" and "W" like a symbol of some bygone optimism.

Metal creaked as he pried.

Once.

Twice.

A final jerk, and the emblem came free with a soft *pop*, one that seemed to echo louder than it should've.

He turned it over in his gloved hand. Inspected it front and back. Then tucked it into his coat like a calling card. Something useful. Something personal.

Behind him, the motel pulsed with low light and static noise. The figures in 109 hadn't stirred. Their blinds stayed drawn, the curtain bent inward like a frozen breath. But he didn't look at them. Not yet.

He walked along the edge of the lot, shadow swallowing shadow as he passed the final rooms. His gait never changed. The rain softened around him, seemed to *adjust* to his pace. He passed a and ignored the vending machine's blank stare, turned the corner at the edge of the building.

The back of the motel was darker. No lights. Just the orange glow of distant city spill across the clouds, and the greenish moonlight glancing off metal trash cans and rotted siding.

He paused at the rear corner of the unit. Glanced once toward the row of bathroom windows, small, high, fogged with years of steam and silence. The curtain in 109 was motionless.

He stood perfectly still.

Not waiting.

Just… pausing.

The next movement had already been decided, he was giving it a moment to arrive.

***

Inside the dark room, the TV clicked on with a plastic snap. Blue light spilled into the room.

At first, they didn't notice it, not really. Just post-coital haze and static. The man reached lazily for the remote, propped on an elbow, the woman pulling the thin sheet back up over her hip. But when the screen lit, it didn't flood the room. It *stopped* short. Something was blocking it.

A shape.

A man.

Seated in the motel's single chair. Silent. Unmoving. Facing them, but not quite. Head slightly down. His outline swallowed the TV's glow, a hunched silhouette, motionless in front of the set like he'd been watching the same frame for hours.

The man sat up sharply. "What the—"

The woman gasped. "How long have you—" she began, but her voice caught before the words finished.

She reached for the lamp.

"Don't," came the reply.

It wasn't loud. But it was *final.*

She froze mid-motion.

The figure shifted, slightly, then leaned forward. The blue flicker caught the edges of two round eyeglass lenses and a single glint of silver, tooth number seven, illuminated in the dark like a coin catching firelight.

He reached into his coat and pulled out a pistol, long, dark, unmistakable: a Luger. He held it comfortably, like a tool he had employed many times in the past.

Then came the suppressor.

He threaded it on slowly. No hurry. No strain. Just patient turns of metal against metal, a clockmaker restoring silence. Click. Click. Tight. Done.

He set the weapon gently on the counter beside him.

From his other pocket, he removed something else, flat, shiny, segmented chrome.

The emblem.

The old kind.

V O L K S W A G O N

He laid it across his lap like a craftsman measuring materials.

Then he spoke. Low. Controlled. An accent that gave every syllable more weight than it needed.

"Five marks a week," he said, "you must set aside... if in your own car you wish to ride."

Neither of them moved.

"In the Reich," he said slowly, voice low and accented, "they called it *Volkswagen*. The people's car. Built not for pride... not for joy... but for survival."

He produced a pair of wire cutters from inside his coat. Old, blackened. Touched by time.

He began snipping.

Clip.

The V hit the motel carpet.

"Built for peasants. For those clinging to existence. For the small."

Clip.

The O.

"The strong do not buy what they cannot earn. But the weak... they find ways."

Clip.

The L.

Then the K. The S. Each with the same clean, surgical motion. They landed with soft taps. Cold metal on thin carpet.

"Wagen," he muttered. "Wheels. Movement. Escape."

He clipped those too.

N.

O.

G.

A.

One letter left.

The **W**.

He held it up in the pliers.

Turned it slowly. Examined it like a surgeon about to begin.

Then he lit the lighter.

It was square, stainless steel, dented at one corner. When the flame caught, it threw a flicker of orange across his glasses, casting brief fire in his eyes.

He lowered the W into the flame.

"You lie beside him," he said, voice unchanged. "A man with no moral character. No redeeming qualities. Not even the good sense to lie well."

The woman began to cry, softly.

"A parasite," he continued, "no different than those that burrow into flesh to feed off the host, not from need, but instinct. Filth feeding on filth. And yet here you are. Beside him. On purpose."

The W began to glow.

Orange-red, then deeper. A ring of smoke rose from its edges.

"Perhaps it is money," he said. "Or the promise of riches. Imagined. Or stolen. The means are unimportant. Only the end."

He stepped forward, Luger in his left hand, the glowing W in the right.

The woman scrambled backward against the headboard. "Please—don't—what do you want—"

He ignored her.

"There is a word," he said, "for a woman like this."

He raised the W in the pliers, holding it like a branding iron.

"In Proverbs, it is written: *A whore may be had for a loaf of bread.*"

The woman screamed.

He said nothing.

"This is our first meeting," he added, stepping to the foot of the bed. "I have never hurt a woman before."

He paused.

Then, coldly: "But if you are with him, when I find him again, you will perish."

"And for the rest of your days, you shall bear the mark of a whore."

Her hands flailed up in defense, her mouth pleading.

He reached forward, seized her by the hair.

She shrieked.

And in one final motion, he pressed the red-hot W to her forehead.

The sound was immediate: a sharp, spitting *hiss*. Her scream ripped the room in half.

The man lunged toward her, too late, too slow.

Big Shoe pivoted and brought the butt of the multitool down hard on his philtrum with a loud, *wet* crack.

The man fell.

The woman convulsed on the bed, her hands scrabbling at the burn, the glowing W now seared into her flesh like the righteous seal of judgment delivered without appeal.

Big Shoe stood motionless.

Then turned.

Walked to the open door.

Did not run.

Did not speak.

Did not close it.

Rain spilled in from the parking lot. And into the parking lot her screams and moans filtered into a night where no one responded, no one cared.

Chapter 15: The Divide

The motel room smelled like blood, alcohol, an off-brand ointment and worst of all, burnt flesh. This had weight. Sour, metallic, thick in the air like something that had soaked into the walls overnight and wasn't planning to leave.

On the nightstand sat the Volkswagen "W," still curled at the edges, its chrome tarnished from heat. Bits of blackened skin clung to the back, flaked and stuck to the edges where the steel had kissed flesh. It looked obscene lying there in the daylight, like a relic pulled from a ruined church.

A Walgreens bag lay crumpled on the floor beside the bed, its receipt poking out like a dead tongue. Scattered across the covers were the spoils of panic: gauze pads, burn cream, antibiotic ointment, alcohol swabs, medical tape, adhesive bandages, even children's Tylenol, maybe grabbed in the blur of purchase. There were no instructions. No plan. Just items with hopeful labels and hollow promises.

The woman lay propped against the headboard, a damp cloth pressed lightly against her forehead. The imprint was unmistakable, a raw, raised W seared into the center of her skin. It wept pus at the edges and pulsed red around the burn. You could already tell it would scar. The shape was perfect.

The man sat on the edge of the bed beside her, fumbling with a small tube of cream. His left cheek was swollen, purplish and shiny under the eye. The spot where the multitool had struck him, the philtrum, was tender and split, with a small scab already forming. Every movement of his upper lip made it throb.

He squeezed the cream onto his finger, then dabbed it carefully onto her brow. She winced but didn't speak.

The silence between them wasn't warm. It was the kind that formed after something irreversible, the kind you didn't break unless you had to.

"I think it's starting to blister," he said finally, low.

She didn't respond.

"Which is good," he added. "Means it's starting to heal."

He dipped gauze into a shallow plastic cup of warm water. Dabbed again.

Her voice came out thin. "He sat there. In the dark. Watching us."

The man froze for half a second, then resumed cleaning.

"How long do you think he was there?"

"I don't know."

"He could've killed us."

"But he didn't."

She turned her head slightly, just enough to look at him with one eye.

"He didn't have to," she said. "He already knew."

The man looked away, toward the table, where the Luger had sat the night before. It was gone now, along with the man who brought it.

"You don't get it," she whispered.

He stood up, tossing the damp gauze into the trash. "No. You don't get it."

She blinked, waiting.

"He's not a ghost. He's not some phantom from hell." He gestured to the room. "He broke in. He left. He's just a man."

She looked down at her hands. One trembled slightly.

"He knew where we were," she said. "He knew what room. He knew what car to pull it off of. He knew how to get in without waking us. He knew when we'd be most vulnerable. That's not—" She paused. "That's not normal."

The man turned, grabbed a clean bandage, and tore it open. The smell of fresh gauze filled the air, sharp like new cloth in a hospital hallway.

"You're letting him get in your head," he muttered.

She looked up at him. "He *branded* me."

He didn't respond. Just gently pressed the gauze against her forehead, then began wrapping medical tape around the edges. It looked makeshift. It *was* makeshift. They weren't doctors. They were barely adults.

After a moment, she spoke again.

"You think he's still watching us?"

"No," the man said. "He got what he wanted."

She didn't believe that. Neither did he. But someone had to say something.

The rain had stopped outside, but the pavement still gleamed through the window slats. Someone's muffler rattled in the distance, a coughing engine wheezing to life, then pulling away. The rest of the lot was still.

"I can't go anywhere like this," she said. "I look like…"

He sat back down beside her. "I know."

She reached for the tube of burn cream. Her hand shook. He took it and applied it for her.

After a long pause, she said, "We have to split up."

He nodded. "I was thinking the same."

"You're the target," she said. "I was just…"

She trailed off.

"Collateral," he finished.

"No," she whispered. "I *chose* this. I chose you. That makes it worse."

He didn't argue. He couldn't.

"You go east," she said. "I'll head back once I know it's safe."

"No," he said. "Other way. I'll go west. Far. Other side of the country. Somewhere with palm trees or neon signs or no last names. I'll get a room. Get a job. Change my hair. Something."

"And me?"

"You go home. Lay low. Lock the doors. Don't use your name for anything. Keep your face covered until that…" he trailed off, gesturing vaguely toward her forehead, "until it fades. If it fades."

"It won't."

He didn't say anything.

"I'll wait to hear from you," she said.

He nodded. "Every couple days. I'll call."

"No names," she said.

"Agreed."

They both stared at the wall for a moment. The buzzing of the TV filled the space, some morning cartoon playing for no one, its colors bleeding into the room's stale palette. A pink dog barked. A laugh track rolled through canned applause.

The man stood and crossed to the table. He picked up the W.

He turned it over in his hand, the edges still blackened, bits of flesh dried against the backside like flakes of meat clinging to a grill grate.

He held it for a moment longer, then set it back down gently.

"I'm buying a gun," he said.

She didn't look up.

He kept talking, like he was reminding himself.

"Something with some power. A magnum. Hollow points. Not that pawn shop shit."

Her voice came out hoarse. "You think that'll matter?"

"If he's flesh and blood…" he said. "Then yeah. It'll matter."

She looked up at him, eyes rimmed red but steady. "What if he's not?"

He didn't answer. Just walked into the bathroom, ran cold water over his hands, and stared at himself in the mirror, bruised, swollen, aging by the hour.

Behind him, her voice carried softly through the doorframe:

"Make sure you know how to use it."

***

The morning sun didn't do the place any favors. It just peeled back the darkness and left everything bare.

The motel lot was mostly empty now, a few cars parked crooked, puddles half-evaporated, oil slicks dried into flaky rainbows. The vending machine buzzed like it always did. A breeze kicked through the gap between buildings, pushing yesterday's trash into new corners.

He closed the trunk of the sedan, a tan, ten-year-old Chevy.

She stood a few feet away, hoodie up, scarf pulled tight around her head. Beneath the gauze taped to her brow, the imprint. The swelling hadn't gone down. The scarf helped. Not much.

Beside her sat a soft-sided overnight bag, zipped halfway, handles knotted from years of use. She hadn't packed much.

"You sure about this?" he asked.

She didn't answer right away. Then: "You said we needed to split up."

He nodded once. "Bus leaves in twenty minutes."

She looked out across the lot. "I'll be back in Berwyn by dark."

He glanced toward the Chevy. "Then I'm gone by noon."

No one said anything for a bit. The wind moved between them like a third presence.

She adjusted her scarf slightly, wincing as the gauze shifted underneath. "What if they ask?"

"Say it was a grease burn," he said. "Say it happened at work."

"They won't believe that."

"Then say you don't want to talk about it."

She pulled her sleeves down over her hands. "I don't."

He nodded, then stepped closer and handed her a small roll of bills. "For cabs. Or whatever."

She took it. Didn't look at the amount. Didn't thank him either.

He looked her over once more — her posture stiff, face half-hidden, eyes swollen from a night with no sleep. There was a smell coming off her skin — antiseptic and gauze and something burned underneath.

"You'll lay low?" he asked.

She gave a dry laugh. "What do you think?"

"No bars. No phone calls. No stories."

"I remember."

He hesitated. "Use cash only."

"I know."

"And if you see anything—"

"I disappear."

He paused. "I'll call in three days. From somewhere west."

"West of what?"

He gave a vague shrug. "Just west."

She looked like she might say something else but didn't. She picked up her bag and slung it over her shoulder. Her movements were careful. Controlled. Like someone protecting a fracture.

They walked to the car together. He opened the passenger door for her. She didn't say thank you, but she paused a moment before getting in.

"You're still gonna buy it?" she asked.

He met her eyes. "Yeah."

"You know how to use it?"

"I'll figure it out."

She gave him one last look, not soft, not angry. Just... final. Then she got in and shut the door.

The drive to the bus station took ten minutes. Neither of them spoke. The radio stayed off.

When they arrived, he pulled up to the curb, let the engine idle. The lot was half-full. A few people milled around the bench under the awning, smoking or staring off.

He popped the trunk. Got her bag.

She adjusted her scarf again before stepping out. The morning light wasn't bright, but it was honest. He could see the sweat on her temple, the rawness under her eyes. She looked like someone coming back from surgery. Or war.

He handed her the bag and looked at her a long moment.

She looked away.

"You'll call?" she asked, still not meeting his eyes.

"I said I would."

"That doesn't mean you will."

He paused. "I will."

She gave a small nod, then turned toward the doors.

He watched her walk inside.

Didn't follow.

Didn't wait.

He got back into the car, adjusted the rearview mirror, and looked at himself for the first time since the bathroom. The bruising had deepened. His cheekbone was swollen. A small crack in his top lip had reopened.

He touched it gently. Winced.

Then he turned the key, pulled out of the lot, and headed west, not because it was safe, but because it was wide, expansive, distant.

Chapter 16: False Peace (Lordsburg)

Lordsburg didn't announce itself. It just appeared, low and tired, crouched in the distance like it had been waiting for him to run out of road.

He drove in late morning, the sun already high, hammering down on the cracked windshield. The town shimmered ahead in the heat, the kind of wavering illusion that made you doubt your own eyes. There was a rusted sign on the outskirts, crooked and sun-faded, that once read *Welcome to Lordsburg*. The welcome was long gone.

Main Street ran a straight line through the center, wide enough for trucks, empty enough for ghosts. A few buildings stood like they'd been forgotten mid-collapse — gas stations with hand-painted prices, one-level motels where the curtains never moved, a pawn shop with bars on the outside. Dust collected in corners and never left.

He slowed as he passed the train tracks. There was no crossing arm, just a sun-bleached *STOP LOOK LISTEN* sign leaning like it had given up. Beyond that, the land opened back up into nothing, just sand, scrub, and a horizon that never got closer.

He pulled into a gravel lot beside a small motel, *Desert View Inn*, though there was no view and barely an inn. The office was a modular shack with a bell taped to the doorframe and a sun-warped poster advertising an extinct brand of soda. A man in a white undershirt sat inside behind a fan, motionless until the door creaked.

"You lookin' for a room?" the man asked, not moving from his stool.

"Yeah. Couple nights."

The man nodded like that was the right answer.

"Fifty-five a night. Cash only."

He paid for three. No ID was requested. The clerk handed him a real key, not a card, attached to a blue plastic tag with "Room 8" melted into it.

Room 8 was around back, tucked away behind a sagging privacy fence and a collection of broken patio chairs. The AC unit in the window was humming already, spitting out air that smelled like wet copper and old socks. He stepped inside.

The room was beige. Not painted beige, *beige*, like everything had once been another color and time had pressed the hue out of it. One bed. One chair. A TV bolted to the dresser, screen slightly crooked. A remote that didn't work until you slapped it. The kind of place people stayed when they didn't want anyone asking why.

He sat on the bed and listened to the fan rattle. The noise was comforting in the way engines are comforting, steady, numbing, predictable. Outside, a stray dog barked once, then stopped.

Later, he walked down the block to a diner that didn't have a name on the sign. Just "OPEN" in flickering red neon. Inside, three old men sat at the counter nursing coffee. Nobody spoke. The waitress was maybe fifty, maybe seventy, skin like cracked leather, eyes yellowed from years of nicotine and suspicion.

He ordered a cheeseburger and water. Ate quietly. Didn't ask for a menu. Didn't look up when she dropped the check.

No one asked where he came from. No one cared. That was why he chose it.

He wandered later, on foot, past a hardware store that hadn't restocked in years, a laundromat with one working machine, and a mural that once depicted a cattle drive but had since flaked away into anonymous shapes. Everything here was slowly becoming something else. Or nothing.

He passed a feed store with a bulletin board nailed to its wall. A handful of sun-bleached flyers clung to it with brittle pushpins. Lost dogs. Old trucks. One sheet, curled at the corners, read:

Ranch help wanted. Cash. No experience needed.

A number was scribbled in Sharpie. He took it.

Back in Room 8, he turned on the TV. Static at first, then a half-broadcast game show from somewhere in El Paso. The volume fluctuated without warning. People clapped, off-sync with the sound.

He laid down without undressing, arms crossed behind his head, staring at the stained ceiling tile above him.

This wasn't peace. But it was distance. And for now, that was enough.

***

The next morning, he called the number from the feed store flyer. It rang five times before someone picked up.

"Yeah," came the voice on the other end. Rough. Unhurried.

"I'm calling about the job. From the bulletin board."

There was a pause. "You ever worked horses before?"

"No."

"Ever muck a stall?"

"No."

"Ever dig a trench or mend wire?"

"Sure."

"Where you calling from?"

"Desert View Inn."

"You got boots?"

"Yes."

Another pause.

"Come out this afternoon. Directions are at the bottom of the flyer.."

Click.

He arrived at the ranch just past noon. It sat a few miles outside Lordsburg, beyond the main road, past a stretch of barbed fence and dried riverbed. The land flattened out like it had been steamrolled into place. Corrals, water tanks, fence lines that zigzagged toward

118

the horizon. A few cattle. Two horses. Nothing romantic about it.

The foreman was a leathery man named Clay. He wore mirrored sunglasses and a straw hat that might have been twenty years old. His handshake was brief and strong, his inspection quicker than that.

"You'll sleep in the trailer," he said. "You'll eat when the work's done. We pay on Fridays. Cash."

The trailer was parked behind the barn. It had two rooms, both narrow, both hot. The mattress was thin. The toilet leaned when you sat on it. A wasp nest bulged under the awning, but they kept to themselves.

The work started early. Before sunrise. Clay didn't believe in alarms. He tapped once on the trailer door with a knuckle and walked off. If you weren't outside in five minutes, you didn't belong there.

Most of it was manual. Cleaning out stalls. Fixing fence lines. Shoveling rock. Digging post holes. Hauling feed. The kind of work that left your shoulders stiff and your palms raw. He bled from a cracked knuckle the first day and didn't bother bandaging it.

He didn't talk much. Clay liked that. The other two hands were younger, Mexican kids from a few towns over. They spoke to each other in quick, quiet Spanish and didn't ask questions. At the end of the day, they drove home. He stayed behind.

At night, he walked the edge of the property with a flashlight and a cigarette. The flashlight's beam was thin and weak, but he didn't care about what it showed. He just needed to move. The desert made a different sound after sunset. Less dry. Less dead. Coyotes barked in the distance. Insects clicked and popped from the brush. Sometimes he could hear the distant hum of a truck passing on the interstate, like a reminder that something still moved out there.

He ate from cans. Chili, corn, tuna. He didn't cook much. The trailer's stove worked but smelled funny when lit. He used the fridge to keep bottled water cold. His back hurt every night, and every night he told himself that was good. Pain meant sleep came faster.

On the fourth day, Clay handed him a shovel and said the septic line needed exposing. The trench ran fifty feet and had to be two feet deep the whole way. Clay marked the line with stakes and didn't speak again for the rest of the day.

He finished the trench before sunset. Clay said nothing, but left a folding chair beside the trailer that night. The message was clear enough.

The gun arrived the following week. A Colt .357 Magnum, deep blue, heavy in the hand. Six-shot, stainless. He bought it off a man at the edge of town who sold out of the back of his truck behind the auto parts store. No name was exchanged. The gun came wrapped in a rag and handed over with a shrug. A box of ammo followed.

He brought it back to the trailer, unwrapped it slowly, then cleaned it twice. No holster. No safe. Just the revolver wrapped back in the cloth and placed under his mattress. He checked it every night before bed. Opened the cylinder. Spun it. Counted the rounds. Closed it carefully. Set it back.

No one at the ranch knew about the gun. No one asked what was under the bed.

He kept working. Kept sweating. His hands toughened. His lip healed. The bruising on his cheek faded to a dull yellow. His jaw stopped clicking when he chewed. He grew a beard. Not much of one, but enough to shade his face and hide the angles.

Clay kept giving him work. He didn't ask for more. The sun kept rising. The nights stayed quiet.

Sometimes, when the work was done, he'd sit on the trailer step and listen to the wind. He'd look out across the wide empty flat and tell himself the truth in pieces. You made it this far. You're still standing. You're not dead.

That had to count for something.

Chapter 17: The Lurching Silhouette

Three months passed without incident.

No notes. No signs. No visitors.

The sun still rose in the east like it always had. The days still began before dawn, sweat still soaked through his shirt by nine, and the work kept him sore in all the right ways. Clay hadn't fired him. The other two hands still nodded once in the morning and ignored him the rest of the day. That was fine. He preferred it that way.

He still lived in the trailer behind the barn. It still leaned slightly left when he walked across the floor. He still used the fridge for bottled water and the stovetop for nothing. Some nights he sat on the step with his boots off, watching the dust float through the last of the sunlight. When he finished his cigarette, he went inside, checked the revolver, and lay down on top of the covers.

He never turned the TV on anymore. He didn't need it. The silence wasn't heavy like it used to be. It had stopped asking questions.

One Thursday night, after dinner, a can of beans and a slice of bread, he walked three blocks into town and stood at the edge of a gas station parking lot. There was a single payphone bolted to the side of the building, faded blue with a cracked plastic cradle and an old local political campaign sticker in peeling white font.

He dropped in two quarters and dialed a number from memory.

She answered on the third ring.

"Yeah."

"It's me."

She exhaled. "I figured."

Silence stretched a few seconds longer than it needed to.

"You sound tired," he said.

"You sound better," she replied.

Neither one of them commented on the unspoken truth: they had talked before. Enough times to have moved past the shock. Past the apologies. Past the anger. Now it was just survival. Check-ins. Codes. Glances over the shoulder, even through the line.

"You still in the same place?" she asked.

"Yeah."

"Still working?"

"Yeah. Ranch job. Pays cash. Clay's decent. Doesn't ask anything."

She made a small noise. Not quite approval, not quite relief.

"The scar's not healing right," she said, quieter now. "I can still feel it when I sleep."

He shifted the phone to his other ear.

"It'll fade."

"It's not fading."

He didn't argue.

"Are you still... doing it?" she asked. "Checking the gun?"

"Every night."

"Good."

A pause. Wind passed through his end of the line, brushing against the receiver.

"I saw a guy the other day," she said. "In the store. Looked like him. Just for a second."

"Was it?"

"No."

He looked out across the lot. A delivery truck passed on the highway, slow and rattling, dragging a breeze behind it.

"Still want me to stay put?" she asked.

"Yeah. For now."

"How much longer?"

"I don't know."

"Ballpark?"

"Another few weeks."

She didn't answer.

"Maybe a month," he added.

Another beat of silence.

"I dream about him sometimes," she said. "Still."

He didn't ask for details.

"I think it's starting to get to me," she continued. "Being back here. This town."

"Berwyn?"

"Yeah. Everything feels like it's waiting."

"For what?"

She didn't answer.

He rubbed the back of his neck.

"You could still leave early," he said. "Just go. Head west. Wait somewhere nearby."

"No."

"Why not?"

"Because he'd expect that. That's what scared people do."

"You're not scared?"

She paused. "I am. But I'm not moving until I know I'm not walking into something worse."

He nodded, then remembered she couldn't see him.

"You sure you're good?" she asked.

"I'm fine."

"Really?"

He glanced toward the road. "The sky's huge out here. You ever notice that? In the desert. There's just more of it."

She let out a small breath. "Sounds nice."

"It is. You'd like it."

Another pause.

Then, quietly: "Maybe."

They stayed on the line a moment longer. He could hear a TV in her background, low volume. Something sitcom-sounding. A laugh track rolled by like a wave.

"I should go," she said.

"I'll call next week."

"Use a different phone."

"I will."

He didn't say goodbye. Just hung up and walked back toward the trailer. The gravel crunched under his boots in slow rhythm. The wind was picking up, carrying the cold out of the mountains. It would be below freezing by dawn.

Inside, the trailer smelled like dust and sweat and hand-cleaned steel.

He opened the drawer. Unwrapped the Colt .357 from its cloth shroud. Checked the cylinder. Six rounds. Wiped it down with a dry rag. Placed it back under the mattress.

He sat down on the bed and leaned back against the wall.

He had work in the morning. More fence line to walk. Maybe a new calf to tag. The days were filling up. The ache in his shoulders had started to feel earned.

Sometimes, lately, he caught himself thinking maybe it really was over. Not all at once. Not like the movies. But in the slow way a fever breaks. Quiet. Gradual.

He hadn't seen the silver tooth in three months.

Maybe he wasn't coming.

Maybe he'd actually gotten away.

After all, Rockford had been practically in his backyard. Lordsburg was another world entirely, distant, anonymous, desolate. All in the best possible way.

He looked toward the ceiling, breathing slow. A small smile crept across his face. Not joy. Just the recognition of space. A crack in the panic.

The kind of thought that comes right before you stop looking behind you.

When he clocked out that evening, he didn't go back to the trailer. For the first time since he'd started working, he went straight to the bar, no change of clothes, no shower, no pause to check the revolver. He felt confident. Safe, even.

The place was called **The Silver Spur**, though the sun-bleached board above the door still carried the ghost of a Coors logo, its paint peeled to nothing. Locals just called it The Spur, or sometimes just "the place." It sat a mile west of the trailer, off the frontage road where the state highway narrowed to two lanes and the desert began reclaiming the shoulders. A gravel lot out front, a neon Bud sign in the window, and not much else.

Inside, it was dim. One ceiling fan twirled lazily, the kind that creaked every third rotation like a loose floorboard in an old farmhouse. The air was thick with cigarette smoke and sweat, not fresh sweat, but the kind that had seeped into wood over decades. There was a jukebox in the corner with a half-lit panel that glowed just enough to reveal dust on the inside of the glass. It played Merle Haggard, Patsy Cline, the occasional Orbison. Songs about things that didn't work out.

He sat at the bar, third stool from the end. The bartender was a retired lineman with a neck like a tree stump and hands that looked like they could fix a transmission by touch alone. He poured drinks slow and didn't talk unless you did first. That suited him fine.

"Another?" the bartender asked, already reaching.

He nodded. The bourbon was cheap but warm going down. The fourth one felt like forgiveness. The fifth one felt like sleep. Something about the quiet made him feel safe tonight. That was the trick of the desert: it didn't warn you. It just lulled you until your guard dropped. And he had.

Lately, he had stopped looking over his shoulder.

The regulars mumbled to each other from the far table, playing poker with beat-up cards and no real money. One of them laughed like an exhaust leak, high-pitched and wheezing. Another scratched his arm so much you wondered if it was nerves or something worse. Nobody asked. This was a town where pasts went unspoken.

He got up to piss and came back to find his drink refreshed. The bartender gave a small nod. He returned it, sat, and stared at the brown glass, his own vague reflection in the backbar mirror.

He thought about calling her again.

The last one had gone well. They'd kept it short. Logistics mostly. Her voice had steadied since that night. The W was healing, she said. Still tender, but she covered it with gauze and a bandana when she went out. People assumed motorcycle accident or kitchen burn. No one looked too closely.

She wanted to know when she could come out west. He had told her not yet. He was still watching shadows.

But truth was, those shadows had gotten thinner. He hadn't felt watched in weeks. Even stopped checking the revolver every night. It stayed under the mattress, still wrapped in the old flannel shirt, but untouched.

Tonight, he thought maybe the worst was really over.

The jukebox played something slow. A lap steel groaned in the background. He closed his eyes for a moment to enjoy the shred of alcohol induced peace.

Just after 10 PM, he stood up, paid cash, and pushed open the door. The dry air hit him like a whisper. The moon was out, low, fat, pale. Clouds drifted like ash across the sky. His boots scraped against the shoulder gravel as he started walking.

The road back to the ranch curved east and then bent around a low hill, maybe fifty feet tall. Not a mountain, not even a bluff, just a rise in the land worn smooth by time and weather. During the day, you could see clear across it. At night, it became a blind spot.

He didn't mind the walk. The mile back to the ranch gave him time to think. To forget. To uncoil the constant tension in his chest. Each step now felt looser, his breath easier. The moon cast long shadows across the cracked road. His boots found the worn path along the shoulder out of habit.

Crickets hummed in the sagebrush. A lone coyote called in the distance.

As he crested the hill, something changed. A pressure. A tremor, not in the ground, but in the air, like the earth itself had inhaled and was holding its breath.

Then he saw it.

At the far end of the road, back toward town, a figure rising slowly over the hill he'd just left behind. First the head. Then the shoulders. The silhouette of a man too tall, too broad, too uneven.

No streetlamps out here. Just moonlight. That was enough.

The shape continued upward, unraveling in stages. He was moving, but not right. The gait was wrong. A stuttered rhythm. Like one leg belonged to a corpse and the other hadn't figured it out yet. His arms didn't swing. His hands hung low. One shoulder slumped lower than the other, dragging him slightly off-kilter. It was a walk that didn't belong on living men.

The man stopped walking.

His chest tightened.

The silhouette advanced slowly, purposefully. One step, then another. The pause between each footfall exaggerated, mechanical, like he was winding himself up with every movement.

The moonlight slid across the road, and the figure became clearer. A 1960s-style suit, discolored and creased. Too heavy for the desert. The jacket hung oddly, shoulders too square, cuffs too short. A tie knotted too tightly around a thick, pale neck.

It was him.

It was Big Shoe.

"No..." the man whispered. His voice felt foreign in his own throat. "No, no, no..."

Adrenaline spiked in his chest, a heat that spread down his ribs and into his legs. Fight or flight surged, but he did neither. He stood frozen.

How?

He'd changed his name. Changed everything. No one at the ranch even knew where he came from. No photos. No online trail. No bank accounts. Just cash and sweat.

And yet here he was.

Not charging. Not running. Just walking. That slow, deliberate gait. Like death itself had found time for a stroll.

The man turned and started walking fast, back toward the trailer. He didn't run, not yet. That would show panic. And he couldn't afford panic. Not again. His boots clicked faster now. He tried not to look back.

The light unnatural clack of the prosthetic floated on the air.

He turned.

Big Shoe had crested the hill fully now, bathed in cold moonlight. His head tilted just slightly to the left. His mouth didn't move. The silver tooth glinted.

Another step forward.

"I'm here, my boy.....I'm here."

Laughter. Soft. Crooked. Broken a hint of congestion.

The man's jaw clenched.

One mile. One goddamn mile. The trailer wasn't far, just down the slope and through the gate.

He didn't run, but he walked faster, his breath loud in his ears.

Behind him: the irregular scrape of rubber on asphalt, the slow tearing sound of leather soles worn wrong by time and deformity.

Half a mile to go.

He veered off the road, taking the shortcut through the brush. The gravel cracked underfoot. A rabbit darted across his path, vanishing into the mesquite.

The trailer came into view, a pale, rectangular shape squatting in the moonlight like a witness who had seen too much and said too little.

He bolted through the gate, took the steps two at a time, and burst into the trailer.

Inside, the air was still. The gun.

Under the mattress. Wrapped in cloth.

He yanked it free. A Colt .357. Heavy. Real.

He turned toward the door.

Big Shoe was already only steps away.

The man stood in the doorway, gun raised.

"Not this time," he whispered.

Big Shoe stepped through the gate.

"You picked the wrong man," the man growled. "I'm not afraid of you anymore."

Big Shoe said nothing. He walked.

One step. Then another.

The moon cast sharp shadows over his face, glasses dull, one eye cloudy. The suit looked worse up close, like it had been pulled off a corpse and never washed.

Big Shoe reached the foot of the steps.

The man aimed the revolver square at his chest.

"Keep coming, you piece of shit. I'll put you down."

Another step.

He was on the landing now.

" I almost pity you…..You are a stupid man. Weak and foolish by all accounts."

"You're dead," the man hissed, and squeezed the trigger.

Click.

Big Shoe didn't blink.

He squeezed again.

Click.

No...

One more.

Click.

The man stared at the revolver. His chest collapsed into itself.

"You... you son of a bitch..."

Big Shoe tilted his head. The silver tooth caught the light.

"While you were filling yourself with poison, I took the liberty of removing the most important part of the gun, the bullets."

And then he stepped forward, fork raised.

He stepped through the doorway as if entering a sanctuary.

The fork gleamed faintly in his hand, thick, dull-pronged, worn smooth by use. Its shape was wrong. Not quite a kitchen utensil, not quite a weapon. Something in between. Something repurposed. Like the man holding it.

The younger man stumbled backward, still clutching the revolver like it might suddenly change its mind and work. His mouth trembled. He didn't even know what he was saying.

"Back the fuck off. Don't come in here. I swear to God I'll—"

Big Shoe lunged.

The fork punched into the hollow above the collarbone, just inside the slope of the neck, the spot surgeons call the supraclavicular fossa. The prongs sank in with brutal precision, striking the thickest knot of nerves. The man's arm seized, then dropped limp.

A white-hot scream tore loose.
The revolver fell. So did the man.

He landed hard on his back, gasping, eyes wide and wild.

Big Shoe leaned over him.
"Brachial plexus," he said calmly. "A delicate intersection of nerves. The arm will not function again tonight."
The man looked at his own limb, limp and dead across the linoleum. Fingers twitching like they'd been unplugged from the grid.

Then the pain arrived. Not all at once, but in blooms. Pulses. Electric.

Big Shoe did not continue immediately. He stood there, eyes lowered, watching the man suffer. The way some men watched boiling water, waiting to see the first break in the surface.

He knelt.

Then he picked up the revolver from the floor and opened the cylinder, showing it to him.

"Empty," he whispered. "How embarrassing."

He let the revolver clatter to the floor and wiped his hand on his slacks.

Then, slowly, he reached into the inner pocket of his coat and removed a small leather pouch. It was unrolled with care, like a ritual. Inside were tools: blades, picks, the fork. Implements chosen not for efficiency, but for communication.

He selected a longer, thinner prong.

"Did you know," he said, voice steady as ever, "that the ribs float near the bottom? That they do not connect to the sternum? This is important."

He lifted the man's shirt with the tip of the new fork.

The man thrashed, tried to roll. Big Shoe pinned him with a knee to the sternum.

"I will make only small adjustments," he said. Then he slid the fork under the lowest rib and pressed in, not a jab, but a slow invasion.

The man howled.

His body bent up, feet kicking, eyes bulging.

Big Shoe held the fork steady and watched the pain unfurl like smoke.

"Your spine is convulsing," he said matter-of-factly. "Common."

He pulled the fork out slowly, like drawing a truth from a liar. Blood ran down the side of the man's torso, thin but steady. A red ribbon.

The man was crying now. Not just from pain, but shame. Fear. Recognition.

"Why..." he gasped. "Why not kill me…"

Big Shoe rose, wiped the fork again, and selected a third.

"You want death. Zis I understand. I do."

He walked slowly around the man, holding the fork with the quiet reverence of a holy artifact.

"But death," he said, "is a permission slip. An end to memory, to consequence. No. I do not give you that."

The next strike came low, just above the kneecap, angling back toward the popliteal fossa.

The man spasmed.

"You will walk with this pain. You will sleep with it. And when it dulls, I will visit again. And sharpen it."

Big Shoe crouched beside him, calm and close as if consoling an old friend.

"You see, my boy. Some relationships leave scars from invisible wounds. They never heal."

"You have inflicted such wounds." "These are the wounds a coward inflicts."

"You have done so on a gentle woman in return for her kindness."

"I prefer real wounds to flesh and bone."

"Heroic wounds that instill and correct a natural order that societal degenerates like yourself attempt to circumvent."

The man was half-curled now, a broken comma on the floor. One hand pressed over his chest wound, the other leg bent at a sick angle. Blood trailed in half-moons across the floor tiles.

Big Shoe reached down and adjusted his collar. "You have been given the gift of reflection," he said. "Treasure it."

The man looked up at him, glassy-eyed. "You're not human," he whispered.

Big Shoe didn't respond.

Instead, he rose, slowly, and rewrapped his tools. Each implement returned to its place with precision. The roll was tied with a simple knot.

Then he turned toward the door.

He did not rush. Did not look back.

Rain had started again, faint at first. Just a mist on the wind. It caught the light as he stepped outside, his shadow stretching long behind him.

The man lay in the center of the trailer, in blood and silence.

And in that silence, something new settled in, a dread more permanent than pain.
Because he knew Big Shoe wasn't gone.

His view of the trailer faded as he slipped into unconsciousness.

***

Clay spotted it before he even reached the steps.

The screen door hung crooked on one hinge, swaying a few inches with each gust. The main door was open, too, not wide, but enough to notice. And that was enough to put Clay on edge.

He pulled the truck up slow and cut the engine. Sat there for a moment, chewing the inside of his cheek. The morning sun had just cleared the eastern ridge. Warm light across the dust and the trailers. It should've been a quiet start to another quiet day.

Clay got out, boots crunching gravel. The door gave a dry metallic groan behind him.

"Hey," he called, approaching. "You in there?"

No answer.

Another step.

He nudged the screen aside and stepped up onto the landing. Still no sound. No movement. Something was wrong. Clay had seen enough to know the difference between someone passed out drunk and something worse.

He pushed the door open.

It took a second for his eyes to adjust.

There was blood. Not a puddle, a trail. Thin red half-moons and scuffed smears across the linoleum. A revolver on the floor. A shape curled near the far wall.

"Jesus…"

He moved in fast now, crouched beside the man, the new guy, the one who'd worked quiet, kept to himself, no trouble. His face was pale, sweat-slick. One arm bent weird. Blood on the shirt, near the ribs. More blood around the leg. Clay didn't touch anything at first. Just crouched there, assessing.

The guy's eyes opened slowly.

He tried to speak, but only air came out.

"Don't move," Clay said. "You hear me? You stay right where you are."

The guy nodded weakly.

Clay stood and scanned the room. No one else. No sign of a struggle, at least not an active one. Just the aftermath. He pulled out his phone and called for help, not 911, not out here. He called Hector, the ranch foreman, and told him to bring the truck with the first aid kit and radio.

Ten minutes later, Clay and Hector loaded the man into the truck, wrapping his torso with gauze and shirts, whatever they had on hand. He screamed once when they lifted him, then passed out.

They drove to the clinic in town, the only one within fifty miles. Clay kept glancing over at him, watching his chest rise and fall. Hector didn't say much. Just drove fast and kept both hands on the wheel.

No one asked questions at the clinic. That was the unspoken rule out here handle what you can, and don't press what you shouldn't. The nurse looked at the wounds, called for the doctor, and then for more help. Clay gave his name and the man's first name, or the one he'd given, and that was enough.

He stayed long enough to hear the doctor say, "He's lucky. None of the organs were hit directly. A few more hours and he might not have been."

Clay left after that. Drove back in silence. He didn't mention the revolver. Or the screen door. Or the weird feeling he got standing there, like something had happened that didn't quite belong to this world.

Chapter 18: Static in the Line

The following week, after being released from the hospital, he sat on the edge of the bed with a towel pressed to his ribs, the fabric already darkening with blood. His right arm hung uselessly at his side, fingers twitching like an afterthought.

The lamp on the counter flickered against the trailer walls, casting shadows that seemed too tall, too slow.

The trailer was quiet except for the hum of the fridge and the occasional rattle of wind against the windowpanes.

The nurse had done a decent job, considering the tools she had. They'd given him a little morphine at the clinic, but not enough, and nothing to take home. Out here, you either healed, or you didn't.

He stared at the landline on the wall. It was off-white once, now yellowed to a smoker's beige. The cord hung like a noose.

He still had the calling card. Same one he'd used before. Numbers scratched into the back. He didn't need to look. Muscle memory took over.

He stood up slowly, one leg stiff, one arm limp. His whole body felt like a map of mistakes.

He lifted the receiver, punched the card number, then the area code. He waited.

Three rings.

Then four.

Then:

"Hello?"

Her voice was cautious. Not afraid, but alert, like she'd just opened a door with no peephole.

"It's me," he said.

A pause.

Then: "Jesus Christ. I thought you were dead."

"I'm not."

"You disappeared."

"I couldn't call sooner."

"Are you okay?"

"No."

Silence. Then softer: "What happened?"

He didn't answer right away. Just let the quiet stretch. He looked at the gauze across his chest, the blood already seeping again. The dull ache behind his clavicle. The rhythmic throb in his knee like a clock ticking down.

"I was visited."

She understood immediately. "Him."

A nod she couldn't see. "Yeah."

Her breath caught. "How?"

"I don't know. I did everything right. Changed my name. Paid in cash. No one here even knows where I came from."

"Then how?"

"I guess it doesn't matter."

Silence again. Longer this time.

He leaned against the wall, head bowed. "I thought it was over. I really did."

"Tell me what he did."

"No."

"You can't protect me from this. Not now."

"I'm not protecting you. I just... I don't want to say it out loud."

He heard her exhale. Not angry, just worn.

"I'm healing," she said after a while. "The burn still hurts. But not as bad."

"I'm sorry."

"I know."

The fridge clicked off. The hum died. Even the wind seemed to pause.

"I can't stay here," he said. "I thought I could ride it out, but... I think he's always known. About me. About us. Where I'd go. What I'd do next."

"Then we leave."

"No. Not we. Just me. You stay put."

"Bullshit."

"I mean it. You've been through enough."

"And you haven't?"

He didn't respond.

She softened. "So where, then?"

"I don't know yet."

"You must have something in mind."

A beat.

Then: "Tokyo."

"What?"

"It's far. And crowded. And impossible to trace. I've got a contact. Guy I knew from back when I wasn't a walking target. He's been out there for years. Says I can stay with him a while. Lay low. Get my bearings."

"Do you trust him?"

"No. But I don't think he'd sell me out either. He's too proud. And too smart to get involved with this."

"This thing... It won't stop."

"I know."

"And neither will you."

"I just need time. A few months. Maybe longer."

"And then?"

"I don't know. Maybe I disappear for good."

"You already have."

That stung. Because it was true. He wasn't the man she'd first met. Not anymore.

"You'll call again?" she asked.

"I will."

"When?"

"I don't know. But I will."

He could hear her trying to stay calm, but her voice cracked.

"I don't want to be left behind."

"You won't be."

"You already did."

He swallowed hard. "I'm sorry."

"I know." A long pause.

Then:

"Do what you have to do," she said. "But next time... if there is a next time... don't make me guess if you're alive."

Click.

He stood there holding the dead receiver.

Outside, the wind picked up again.

Chapter 19: Corners of the Earth – Tokyo, Japan

The plane began to lower, and through the oval window came the first shape of land, an island crouched beneath gray cloud, speckled with low, shingled rooftops and the suggestion of tide. No golden welcome, no postcard skyline. Just shoreline, muted and calm.

He leaned into the glass, forehead grazing the plastic, watching the coast rise to meet him like a thing summoned.

Here it was. Japan.

He'd been too numb during boarding to believe the plane would even take off, half-waiting for hands on his shoulder or a name called out over the intercom. But the doors had sealed. The wheels had lifted. And now, hours later, the ocean was falling away and the island was rising up, not just land, but *possibility*.

Below, thin rivers traced their way between industrial blocks, green fields folded into themselves like origami, and distant bullet trains slithered quietly along their tracks like brushed steel veins.

He didn't know the names of the cities. He didn't need to. The whole country felt alien enough to promise rebirth.

There was a brief shudder as the landing gear dropped, and then, with a suddenness that startled him, the tires kissed earth. A moment of rubber grabbing asphalt. The body of the plane dipped forward with a sigh, as if relieved to have made it.

He exhaled through his nose. Hands clenched on the armrest, not out of fear, just habit.

As the plane taxied, he closed his eyes. No thoughts of what he left behind. No memories of the fork, the motel, the blood. Just a whisper of hope: *Maybe this time it's enough.*

The seatbelt sign went off. He waited. Always wait. He let the aisle clear. Stood only when the shuffle of bodies had begun to thin.

When the cabin door opened, he stepped into the jet bridge, and the air was wet. Not with rain, but with weight.

It clung to his skin immediately. Thick, summer humidity with a hint of burnt plastic and distant ozone.

But it didn't matter.

He was somewhere else now. And maybe, just maybe, nowhere was exactly what he needed.

***

At Narita Airport, he followed the others out into the corridor, a long glass throat with moving walkways humming beneath bright, white lights.

Signs overhead pointed in three languages, but he didn't need to read them. Everyone moved the same direction, heads slightly bowed, luggage trailing behind them like broken tails.

It was quiet. Not silent, but quiet in a way American airports never were. No shouting. No barking families. Just the soft murmur of rubber soles and suitcase wheels clicking at the seams.

The floor gleamed. The air was cool and dry and artificial. He passed rows of potted bamboo and digital kiosks flashing smiling cartoon mascots. Somewhere near Gate 36, he caught a faint scent of miso and soy from a food stall, but it vanished as quickly as it came, replaced by nothing. The airport smelled like *nothing*. Like a place scrubbed clean of all human evidence.

He liked that.

At immigration, he handed over the forged passport with two hands, he remembered that part. Use both hands. Show respect. The uniformed officer flipped through it without emotion, scanning it, then scanning him.

There was a moment, one breath too long. A delay.

But then the man stamped the page with a neat mechanical motion, slid it back across the counter, and nodded once.

"Arigatō gozaimasu," he murmured, the syllables dry on his tongue.

No alarms. No second glances. No questions.

He kept walking.

***

He followed the signs for the Narita Express, down one escalator and then another. The floor

149

changed from white tile to grey. Cooler underfoot. The air grew heavier, not hot, just dense, like the weight of the country gathered down there, waiting for him.

He bought a ticket from a machine using cash, fingers hovering over the buttons longer than necessary. The touchscreen glowed blue against his skin. When the ticket dropped into the tray, he picked it up slowly, as if touching paper for the first time.

Narita Express to Shinjuku. Track 4.

Signs in English helped, but he followed the current of bodies more than the lettering. A group of tourists veered left toward a ramen shop. A businessman with a suitcase and a surgical mask moved past him like smoke.

When he reached the platform, the train was already there. Red stripe down its side. Sleek. Silent. No motor growl, no hiss of brakes, just presence, like it had always been there and always would be.

The doors opened with a soft mechanical tone.

He stepped in.

The cabin was cool, crisp, perfectly lit. Soft gray seats with red trim. No gum stuck under armrests. No graffiti. No smell of disinfectant trying to mask something worse.

Just clean air. And quiet.

He chose a window seat. Set his bag on the floor. Watched as a uniformed woman on the platform bowed to each car as the train prepared to leave. It was ceremonial, not performance, not PR. Something older. Built into the bones of the place.

The train pulled out exactly on time. No lurch. No warning. Just motion.

Outside, the airport slid away. Then parking lots. Then warehouses. Then green.

Low rice fields blurred past, broken by gray cinderblock homes with rusted balconies and laundry hanging in still air. Power lines sagged low across backyards. Vending machines stood alone on empty corners like forgotten shrines.

He stared at it all like it was a painting. The rhythm of the train steadied his pulse.

For the first time in weeks, he felt his shoulders lower. His jaw unclench.

The thing in the Southwest… that had been real. Too real. But this…

This was something else.

Maybe not freedom. But something near it.

Maybe the city would swallow him whole, and never spit him back out.

Chapter 20: Kabukichō

The train slipped into Shinjuku Station like a thought being buried. No screech, no thud. Just arrival.

Doors opened with a soft *ding*, and the passengers disembarked in quiet procession, no bumping, no sideways glances. Everyone moved with intent, but without rush.

He followed.

The platform stretched wide, ceilings low and ribbed with exposed ducts. Signs blinked in timed sequence, yellow, white, red, directing the flow like blood through arteries. The air smelled faintly of ozone and something sterile beneath it all.

He let the crowd pull him forward.

Up one escalator, then another. A slow drift toward daylight.

By the time he reached the surface, the sun was beginning to drop, not in a blaze, but in a smog-filtered hush. The sky above Shinjuku glowed orange-gray, backlighting a jagged skyline of blinking towers and crooked signage.

It didn't feel like walking into a city. It felt like walking into circuitry.

LED ads danced across glass high-rises, beams of color glancing off steel like oil slicks. Somewhere to his left, a girl in a pink maid costume handed out flyers to no one. To his right, an old man pushed a cart stacked with crates of empty bottles, the wheels squeaking in protest.

There were no horns. No sirens. No shouting.

Only sound, orchestrated and strange. Crosswalks chirped like digital birds. Loudspeakers on the corners broadcasted soft announcements in melodic tones. The crowd moved in rhythm to sounds he didn't yet understand.

Even the chaos was rehearsed.

He stood at the edge of the sidewalk for a long moment before crossing. Just watching.

The people here dressed like they had somewhere to be, even if they didn't. Students in crisp uniforms. Office workers in identical white shirts and black pants. A woman in heels too tall for walking carried a cat in a baby stroller. No one looked out of place. Which meant he didn't either.

That hit him unexpectedly hard.

He could disappear here.

Not in the way he'd disappeared before, behind aliases and motel doors and prepaid burner phones, but really disappear. Into density. Into indifference.

No one here knew his name. No one here cared.

A light changed. The crowd surged forward. He moved with them.

Somewhere in the distance, a train hissed to a stop beneath the streets. A vending machine beside him glowed with cans of coffee and corn soup stacked in perfect verticals. A paper lantern swung gently above a doorway with no sign.

He felt like he was underwater, not drowning, but suspended.

He didn't speak the language. Didn't know the currency by feel yet. Didn't even know which exit to take.

But for the first time in a long time, he wasn't waiting to be hunted.

He was just... walking.

***

The apartment wasn't far. He had the address written on a scrap of paper, block number, building code, something about a second-floor keypad. But he didn't plug it into a map. Not yet. He walked. Wanted to walk.

The station fell behind him, and with it the polished logic of train schedules and station maps. Ahead lay something less ordered, a sprawl of sensory contradiction that kept reshaping itself with each block.

Mirrored skyscrapers stood like silent gods, their surfaces polished so clean they reflected not just light but motion, glass monoliths flickering with shifting sky and swarm. And then, tucked between them: wooden homes with sliding doors, tucked-away shrines with stone steps rubbed smooth by thousands of unspoken prayers.

One shrine sat wedged between a coffee shop and a massage parlor, its red gate sun-faded and crooked. A small paper lantern hung over the altar, trembling in the faint breeze kicked up by passing taxis. A row of ceramic foxes watched from the shadows, their chipped smiles unreadable.

He paused.

People passed him, none of them looked. No one bowed. The shrine was just part of the scenery now, like an old scar the city had stopped noticing.

But to him, it landed.

This city had layers.

Old wood and new steel. Smoke and screens. Ink and neon.

He kept walking.

A billboard above him flashed an ad for contact lenses, the model's eyes so large and bright they seemed to follow him. Beneath it, a cluster of schoolgirls in matching uniforms laughed into their phones. The sound was shrill but honest. He let it pass through him.

Just ahead, a black van rolled slowly through the intersection, moving like a funeral procession. On the roof: two mounted loudspeakers and a broad white banner with bold red kanji. A man's voice boomed from the speakers, urgent, sharp, commanding. He flinched. Instinctively looked behind him.

But the van moved past with all the menace of a parade float.

Campaign vehicle. Political ad. Nothing more.

He let out a breath, short and relieved. Then, unexpectedly, he laughed. Not loudly. Just a breath that shaped itself like laughter on the way out.

This place was insane.

But at least it didn't know him.

He passed a row of shops, tailor, barber, pawn, and each one had signage in overlapping layers, some with hand-drawn brushstrokes, others backlit in harsh plastic light. A tangle of wires sagged between the rooftops like spiderwebs made of black rope.

There were no street corners like home. No neat corners at all. Just angles. Intersections at odd tilts, alleys that split and curled like veins. No two doors were the same height. No window seemed made to match its neighbor.

The streets narrowed.

He turned left at a vending machine selling surgical masks and strawberry water, then right past a building with a crooked karaoke sign blinking one letter at a time — K... A... R... then flickering out.

It was here the city changed again.

The rhythm slowed.

The foot traffic thinned, but the lights grew louder. Signs multiplied in size and saturation. Voices grew softer, but the silence between them felt loaded.

This was Kabukichō.

He knew it before the paper in his pocket confirmed it. You could feel it, not just visually, but in your skin.

Here, everything leaned inward.

Buildings pressed against each other like conspirators. The lights no longer guided, they seduced. And above it all, barely visible from the street, surveillance cameras blinked like tired eyes.

This wasn't where tourists came for temples.

This was where you disappeared.

And somehow, that suited him just fine.

***

The deeper he walked, the more the air seemed to change, not temperature, but texture. Thicker. Like he had passed through some invisible veil that divided Tokyo into two halves: one that functioned, and one that *absorbed*.

Kabukichō didn't pulse with life. It whispered.

Hostess bars stood behind tinted glass, their entrances flanked by flower arrangements that looked fresh until you got close. He passed a group of girls in platform heels and padded bras standing under a glowing sign that simply read "New Club Purity" in looping pink script. They barely looked eighteen. One adjusted her hair in a mirrored panel next to the door. Another stared down with dead eyes and perfect eyeliner.

He kept walking. Head down. Not out of fear, out of respect. You didn't look too long at anything here. Not if you wanted to stay invisible.

The sidewalk narrowed. A stack of rusted bicycles leaned against a concrete wall painted with cartoon sushi characters. Beside them, a bent sign on a folding stand read "Men's Aroma" with an arrow pointing up a dark stairwell.

He checked the slip of paper again. Block 1-18, Building 3, Room 2B. Second floor, above a bar called "Lily."

He passed Building 1. Then 2. The numbers weren't in any order that made sense. Some were carved into cement, others printed on stickers peeling at the corners. It took ten minutes of doubling back and counting mailboxes before he found it, tucked behind a stack of yellow Kirin crates and a faded poster for a long-closed steakhouse.

The bar below was open. The name **"Lily"** glowed in cursive pink above the door, but one of the letters had burned out. From inside, he heard muffled voices, two men laughing, something clinking against glass, and a short burst of piano keys from a karaoke track.

A narrow staircase beside the door led upward. Concrete steps. Damp air. The smell of mildew and perfume.

He climbed. Slowly.

There was no handrail. A security camera was mounted above the landing but pointed away, either broken or never wired to begin with.

At the top of the stairs, he found a gray metal door with a keypad next to the handle.

He took the slip of paper from his pocket again.

Code: 7-2-9-9-4-3

He pressed the digits. The buttons were soft and slightly sticky, like they hadn't been used in months.

The lock clicked. A low mechanical whir.

He pushed the door open.

The apartment was smaller than he expected.

Ten feet across, maybe. The ceiling low enough that he ducked out of instinct, even though he didn't have to.

One window, covered by a vinyl blind with a broken cord. The air was stale, with an undercurrent of mold and kitchen grease. Somewhere behind the wall, a pipe gurgled, the sound of a toilet flushing on another floor.

The floor was laminate tile, curled at the edges from moisture. A futon had been rolled up in the corner. Beside it, a squat table with a chipped ceramic ashtray already half-full.

There was a refrigerator the size of a suitcase humming near the door. A sink with a single rusted faucet. Above it, a cabinet with no handle.

And that was it.

No TV. No desk. No chairs.

Just a room. A box.

But it was his now.

He stepped inside and shut the door behind him.

Locked it.

Then locked it again.

***

He didn't turn on the light right away. Let the dim spill from the hallway fade out behind him, the door clicking shut like the lid of a coffin, one he had crawled into willingly.

For a few seconds, he stood still. Let his eyes adjust. Let the quiet settle in.

No footsteps above him. No neighbors yelling. No muffled TV.

Silence.

Real silence, the kind you can hear.

He dropped his duffel bag onto the floor and crouched beside it, unzipping slowly. Inside: clothes rolled tight, a small pouch of cash, his forged ID tucked between two socks. A paperback novel in English he hadn't read past chapter three. A toothbrush with no case.

He placed the items methodically on the low table. Clothes folded again. Book stacked. Money wrapped in a rubber band and slipped into the ashtray for now.

He didn't open the window. He didn't need air. Not yet.

Instead, he took a breath through his nose, slow and quiet. Sat on the edge of the futon and let his hands hang between his knees.

For the first time in months, there was no sound chasing him. No gears turning in the background of his life.

It didn't feel safe exactly. But it didn't feel hunted.

That was something.

After a while, he stood. Slipped on his jacket and stepped back out, locking the door behind him. Not with panic, just habit.

Down the stairs. Past the karaoke bar, louder now, a man off-key belting out something earnest and tragic. Through the narrow alley, under a tangle of wires that clicked softly in the rising wind.

At the corner, beside a cigarette machine, stood a red vending unit glowing faintly in the dark. A Sapporo logo across the top, half-faded. A cicada buzzed somewhere nearby, invisible.

He slipped coins into the slot, the machine beeped twice, and with two satisfying *clunks*, a pair of tall silver cans dropped into the tray.

He stood there for a moment with them in his hands. Cold metal against warm skin. No reason to rush.

He turned back toward the stairs.

Up. Past the girls outside Club Purity. Past the bent sign for "Men's Aroma."

Back through the keypad door, the hallway, the click of his own lock turning.

Inside. Lights off.

He sat cross-legged on the floor beside the low table and cracked the first can. The hiss was clean and sharp.

He drank slowly.

No TV. No phone. No music.

Just the thrum of his own pulse and the low vibration of the mini-fridge compressor switching on and off.

Halfway through the second can, he stretched out on the floor. One arm behind his head. Eyes on the ceiling.

No plans. No agenda.

The beer warmed in his blood like a blanket.

His breath slowed.

And somewhere between one blink and the next, he fell asleep.

Chapter 21: Settling In

He woke to the smell of warm metal and dust. For a moment, he didn't know where he was. The ceiling above him was bare plaster, cracked in thin spiderweb lines. The hum of the mini-fridge pulsed low and steady.

Then he remembered, Japan.

The cans of Sapporo still sat on the table, one empty, one half-drunk and flat. He drank from it anyway. Warm beer, metallic and bitter. He didn't care.

He stood, stretched, and crossed to the small window. Pulled the blind halfway up.

Morning in Kabukichō.

The alley below was empty except for a delivery cart stacked with crates of Suntory whiskey. A man in a gray jumpsuit unloaded them one at a time, placing each bottle gently as though the glass might bruise. Across the alley, a bar sign flickered on even though the sun was already high.

The air outside shimmered with heat.

He dressed in yesterday's clothes, ran water over his face in the sink, and left the room without a word.

By the second day, he found his rhythm.

The vending machines became his breakfast stop, canned coffee, sweet and black, with a taste like scorched caramel. He'd drink it standing on the curb, watching the tide of office workers spill out of the station. All of them in white shirts, black pants, polished shoes. A uniform city.

He liked the convenience stores, *konbini*, as the sign said. They were clean in a way American corner stores never were. No sticky floors, no sour smell of old mops. Here, even the microwaved pork buns looked like they'd been arranged by hand.

Each morning, he'd buy a hard-boiled egg wrapped in plastic and a rice ball with tuna inside. Then he'd eat it slowly while leaning against a rail near the station, just another foreigner watching the trains glide in and out.

By afternoon, he'd walk. No destination. Just streets.

Tokyo shifted block by block. One minute, you were under mirrored skyscrapers with digital ads blasting from thirty stories high, women with porcelain skin selling bottled water with voices like jingles. The next, you'd find yourself on a narrow backstreet where a tiny shrine stood beside a cigarette shop.

One afternoon, he passed such a shrine, barely wider than a doorway. A small wooden gate, painted red. Paper streamers fluttered gently in the subtle breeze that reached the alley. A few wilted flowers had been left on the steps.

He paused there, just watching.

No one else did. People walked past like it wasn't even there.

For a moment, he felt a strange calm. The shrine had survived glass towers, neon, and greed, it just existed. Quietly.

Maybe he could too.

On his third evening, he wandered farther north and passed a dry cleaner still lit from inside, the hum of tumbling dryers mixed with the quiet shuffle of footsteps behind him. A window display showed crisp white shirts on wire mannequins, sleeves folded just so.

Further along, a boy rode past on a bicycle with a basket full of small packages, the bell on his handlebar chiming softly as he turned a corner.

Lights blinked on above shuttered shops, one by one, like the street was waking from a nap.

The neighborhood changed as the sun dipped. Kabukichō by day was odd, but by night it became something else, a low buzz of desire and transaction, all dressed in lights.

Signs stacked on signs. Pink, blue, gold. Host clubs with photos of airbrushed men staring down like mannequins. Girls in school uniforms handing out flyers they didn't want to hand out. Tall men with sharp suits and sharper haircuts watching from doorways with flat eyes.

He didn't stop anywhere.

Just walked, hands in pockets, breathing it in.

He liked that no one cared. Everyone was busy selling something, buying something, pretending something. He wasn't part of it, but he wasn't outside it either.

For once, he wasn't being chased.

***

He didn't go back to the same streets. That felt like tempting fate.

Instead, each day he picked a new direction, treating the alleys like a shuffled deck, always drawing a different card. He passed storefronts that never opened, doorbells with no labels, rusted mailboxes taped shut.

Somewhere past the third turn, a bakery vented the smell of anise and steam. Elderly women stood outside in visors, chatting softly. He slowed to pass them, but none looked his way. Their conversation continued, sealed in its own language. He may as well have been mist.

At a crosswalk, he stood next to a woman in a full business suit walking a tiny, quivering dog dressed in a sailor costume. She adjusted the leash with perfect composure, as if nothing about the scene was strange. No one stared. No one even noticed.

He started to believe that maybe Japan didn't do *notice*.

Not in the way he was used to. Not in the American way, the constant scanning, posturing, threat assessment in every glance.

Here, everyone was sealed into themselves. And for the first time in years, that seemed like safety.

In the evenings, he stopped at a discount bento shop near the edge of the neighborhood, a little place with

168

bad lighting and faded food photos taped to the walls. They had boiled eggs steeped in soy, cold fried chicken, and salmon cutlets wrapped in cling film. Everything was slightly too salty, slightly too cold, and exactly what he needed.

He liked the old man who ran the register, face carved like driftwood, voice barely above a whisper. Never asked questions. Just slid the change across the counter with two fingers and a nod.

One night, the man slipped a packet of pickled daikon into his bag and muttered, "Service."

That stuck with him.

Back at the apartment, he'd eat sitting on the floor with his back against the wall, a tall can of beer in one hand and a pair of warped plastic chopsticks in the other.

The light above the sink buzzed faintly but never flickered. The hum of the fridge had begun to feel like company.

He'd chew slowly, scroll through the English pages of the newspaper he'd picked up from the station kiosk, then fold it perfectly and slide it under the futon. It became ritual.

Afterward, he'd smoke out the window, watching the alley darken. Sometimes he'd see a cat hop a fence. Sometimes nothing at all.

The city didn't seem interested in him. And that, that *indifference*, was the first mercy he'd been given in a long time.

One night, lying flat on the futon in his undershirt, a cold can in his hand, he whispered aloud just to hear his own voice.

Not a prayer. Not a confession.

Just words.

"I'm not dead."

It surprised him. Not the words, the sound.

They sounded hollow. Uncertain.

He laughed once, just under his breath, and took another sip.

***

He found the bathhouse by accident.

Tucked behind a florist and a coin laundry, down an alley no wider than a parking space, a painted wooden sign, warped from sun and rain, with steam curls rising from red brushstrokes:

銭湯 – Public Bath

He stood in front of it a moment, unsure. Then stepped inside.

The lobby was small and clean. White tile floor. A cracked vending machine humming near the entrance. Behind a yellowed counter sat an old woman in a navy apron, eyes half-lidded, fanning herself with a folded magazine.

She didn't look up.

He pointed at the sign on the wall.

"One?" he said.

170

She nodded. Took his yen. Slid him a key on a coiled plastic bracelet.

No small talk. No questions. Just the way he liked it.

The men's changing room was silent except for the soft squeak of feet on tile. A row of low lockers, each numbered in fading gold. Wooden benches polished smooth by years of damp skin. The air smelled like cedar, soap, and rusted metal.

He undressed slowly, folding his clothes the way he'd seen others do.

No one stared. No one spoke. The few men inside moved like ghosts — rinse, scrub, soak, dry. Everyone knew their place. Everyone observed the same unspoken rhythm.

He stepped into the shower area. A wall of stools, plastic basins, handheld mirrors.

He sat.

He scrubbed.

He rinsed.

He did it again, just to be sure.

When he stepped into the main bath — a rectangular pool sunk into stone tile — the heat climbed his legs like smoke. He eased in slowly, lowering himself one vertebra at a time.

When the water reached his collarbone, he exhaled.

The steam softened everything. His face. His thoughts. The ache behind his eyes.

He closed them.

He didn't think about the motel. Or the fork. Or the woman screaming in the parking lot.

He didn't think about Big Shoe.

He thought about nothing.

Just the warmth.

Just the quiet.

He stayed until his skin began to pucker and his limbs felt boneless. When he finally rose, the air outside the bath slapped him with a cold hand. He dressed without a word. The old woman at the counter was asleep now, chin tucked into her collarbone.

He left without waking her.

Outside, the air was thick with early night. The alley buzzed with a single blue mosquito lamp above the laundry. He could hear jazz coming from a second-floor window nearby — old stuff, brushed snare and soft trumpet. Something kind.

He walked back slowly.

Feet light. Towel draped around his neck. A cold drink in a bag swinging from his wrist.

For the first time in a long time, he didn't feel like someone who had *escaped*.

He felt like someone who had *arrived*.

Chapter 22: Phantom Glimpse

The ramen had been perfect, hot, greasy, loaded with garlic. He sat at the counter long after the bowl was empty, sipping slowly from the last of the broth like it meant something. His legs were sore from walking all day. His shoulders ached from carrying nothing. But inside, he felt calm.

For weeks now, Tokyo had held him. Not gently, it wasn't that kind of place, but securely, like a city gripping you just tight enough to make sure you stayed in motion.

The old man behind the counter gave a nod as he stood to leave. No words. Just the nod. He liked that.

He stepped outside and the door clicked shut behind him, cutting off the kitchen's steam and fluorescent hum. The night air met his face with a cool slap. Not cold, just enough to pull the skin a little tighter.

He lit a cigarette and stood there a moment, letting the warmth of the meal settle into his chest. Neon buzzed above. A sign flickered red, then steady again. Somewhere nearby, a siren wailed low and far, the way all sirens did in this city, like they were ashamed of interrupting.

He turned the corner.

And stopped.

Across the street, maybe thirty feet away, just beyond the vending machines and a parked delivery bike, someone was walking.

No — *not walking.*

Moving.

Tall. Wrong.

The figure stepped into the edge of a crowd waiting at the crosswalk. And for a moment, just one, the bodies parted. And there it was.

A *gait.* Slight but unmistakable.

Right leg lagging. Left shoulder rising half a beat early to compensate.

A rhythm that wasn't rhythm. A walk that was half-step, half-drag.

His stomach flipped.

The figure wore a coat, tan or maybe brown, couldn't tell under the streetlight. The back of a head, short hair, graying. The shape was right. The slope of the neck. The angle of the jaw.

And then the crowd surged again, someone laughed, a scooter rattled past, and the figure was gone.

He blinked.

No — not gone. *Just not there.*

The crosswalk changed. People moved. The bike engine faded. The vending machine hissed as someone bought a bottle of green tea.

He stood frozen, cigarette burning in his fingers.

Across the street, the sidewalk was empty.

He scanned the shops, the alley behind the bike, the corner where the man might have turned. Nothing.

No one was running. No one was watching.

Just another Tokyo night.

He stayed there longer than he meant to, breathing through his nose, letting the noise of the city settle back around him like dust.

His pulse slowed.

He took one last drag and flicked the cigarette into a drain.

It wasn't him.

It couldn't have been.

I'm just seeing what I expect to see.

Still, he walked home a different way.

***

The next morning, he woke early, earlier than usual. The sun hadn't fully cracked the alley yet, but the room was already warm. He lay there for a while, staring at the ceiling, trying to remember if he'd dreamed anything.

Nothing. Just static.

By the time he stood up, the room was already filling with the scent of someone else's cooking, garlic, maybe soy. The bar downstairs must've been prepping early. He washed his face in the sink, pulled on a clean shirt, and decided to go out without a plan.

No errands. No agenda. Just walk.

He ended up in Yoyogi Park by accident, one train ride and three wrong turns later.

The trees were wider here. The air cooler. Pigeons fought over breadcrumbs beneath a wooden bench. Elderly men fed stray cats from paper bags, muttering softly in the dialect of people who didn't care to explain themselves.

Near the center of the park, a boy, maybe high school age, was playing the violin with cracked fingers and a rental amp. The sound was jagged at first, unsure of itself. But it caught rhythm eventually. Something mournful and sharp. Not classical. Not street pop. Something in between.

He sat on a bench, arms folded, and watched.

No one else stopped. That was fine. The music wasn't meant to draw a crowd.

It was meant to exist.

When the boy finished, he bowed once, not to anyone, just to the ground, and packed the violin into a case lined with a bright red cloth.

The man stood. Walked over. Dropped a 500 yen coin into the open case.

The boy looked up, surprised, and nodded with both hands.

No words exchanged. None needed.

Chapter 23: Bunraku and Panic

He was three blocks from the apartment when he heard the drumming. Soft, quick, the kind that sounds playful at first, then too sharp on the second beat.

People were gathered at the edge of a small plaza, standing in a rough semicircle. Some sat on crates or the curb. Others leaned on bikes.

Above the heads, he saw it, a miniature stage built into the bed of a flatbed truck. Red cloth, bamboo poles, a banner with faded kanji flapping against the cab. Strings looped from a frame above, taut and waiting.

Bunraku.

Traditional puppet theater. He'd seen photos once, lacquered masks, silk robes, three handlers cloaked in black. He remembered it as quaint. Old-world.

He stopped at the edge of the crowd, took a spot beside a man eating cup noodles, and watched.

The puppet on stage, a traveling peasant, was fumbling with a pack tied to its back. Two operators, dressed in black and hooded, moved it in smooth, exaggerated gestures. One handled the legs and torso. The other, arms and head.

The coordination was perfect.

Each step a study in control. Each tilt of the head somehow sad and funny at once.

The crowd chuckled when the puppet tripped and spilled rice across the stage. Someone behind him said something in Japanese and laughed softly. Children near the front clapped their hands.

He smiled. Just a little.

The next puppet entered, a samurai. Towering. Proud. One handler manipulated the drawn sword, angling it downward as the puppet bowed in rigid ceremony.

The peasant puppet backed away, trembling. The movements were tight, jerky — shoulders hiked, arms quivering. There was a rhythm to it.

Something in the way it **hesitated**, then **lurched**, then **snapped its head sideways**—

His smile dropped.

A chill slid up the back of his neck.

The puppet stumbled, turned, and tried to flee. The samurai stepped forward, one hard foot, then the other.

Then. clean, efficient, the **sword plunged forward**.

Right into the peasant's chest.

The puppeteers were flawless: the wounded puppet reeled, arms splaying, knees buckling. It collapsed precisely, the limbs folding in on themselves like paper. A perfect, practiced fall.

Just like the substation.

He could see it again, the way the man jerked when the fork hit the shoulder, that moment of slackness before the scream. The way his body dropped, not like a man, but like a thing.

The crowd laughed again, a sudden rise of voices.

He couldn't breathe.

The heat around him thickened. The smell of sweat, soy sauce, the oil from the noodles. The sound of the puppets. The drum. The string tension.

He stepped backward. One foot. Then another. His legs felt weak and trembled as adrenaline pulsed through his chest.

No one noticed.

He turned.

Walked. Fast. Eyes forward. Not running. Just **moving**.

A block away, the drumming still echoed faintly behind him.

By the time he reached the apartment, he was slick with sweat. Not from heat. From memory.

He punched the keypad wrong the first time. Then again.

Third try, the door clicked open.

He stepped inside. Shut it. Locked it. Stood with his back to it, chest rising and falling like he'd run five miles.

The silence hit like a wave.

Still shaking, he walked to the sink. Ran cold water over his hands. Let it spill over his wrists, watching the beads trace veins.

"Just nerves," he whispered.

No one there to hear it.

"Just nerves."

He stood there a long time. Breathing.

And eventually… the panic passed.

"Just nerves."

He wiped the water from his face, crossed the room, and sat down at the table.

Stared at the phone card.

Then picked up the receiver.

The phone card worked on the first try.

She answered after two rings. "Hello?"

"It's me."

Silence. Then breath. Then, "You're okay."

"I'm okay."

"How's it feel?"

He looked around the room. The table. The fridge. The towel still drying on the doorknob.

"Like I'm not anywhere. Which is good."

She didn't laugh. But he could feel her almost smile.

"I'll call again in a few days," he said. "It's easier now."

"All right."

Before she hung up, she said, "Just stay gone."

He nodded, though she couldn't see it. "That's the plan."

Chapter 24: The Second Sighting

It was late afternoon when he boarded the train, not quite rush hour, but close. The sun hung low in the sky, caught between the buildings like something too heavy to rise or fall.

He slipped into a seat near the rear of the car, set his bag between his feet, and leaned back. The vinyl was warm. The cabin smelled faintly of old air conditioning and newspaper ink.

His eyes were dry. He hadn't slept much. Not poorly, just shallow, like skimming across water, never fully sinking.

The doors stayed open longer than usual. The conductor's voice buzzed over the speaker, low and garbled.

Across the tracks, another platform. Another train that wasn't coming. Just space. People. Movement.

And then:

Stillness.

A shape.

One figure.

Far side of the platform. Standing alone. No motion.

No phone. No bag. No newspaper.

Just… standing.

Brown suit.

Wide shoulders.

Head tilted slightly forward.

And those shoes —

God.

Those shoes.

The left one heavier. The stance offset, familiar in the worst way.

Not turned toward the train.

Turned toward *him*.

The space between them should have been comforting, a full track, two platforms, two cities, two lives. But it wasn't. It felt compressed. Crushed down to nothing.

His throat tightened.

He blinked.

Still there.

The train doors chimed.

Still there.

He turned slightly, not wanting to seem obvious, but he had to know, had to see the eyes. But the figure didn't move. Didn't tilt. Didn't sway.

Just watched.

Just waited.

No one else on the train reacted. The girl beside him scrolled her phone. An old man read the paper. Two kids laughed softly over something on a screen.

Nobody noticed.

Not even a glance.

The doors closed.

And the train began to move.

Not fast. Just enough.

The platform began to slide past.

He looked back.

Big Shoe remained still.

No effort to follow. No shift in posture. Just an anchor. Unmoving. Watching him leave.

It felt like a dream.

The kind you forget until a week later when something small, the light, a sound, a shape, brings it screaming back.

The train pulled into a curve. The platform disappeared.

And he was still staring out the window, long after there was nothing there.

The train moved through the tunnel, lights flickering rhythmically against the windows. He stayed in his seat, staring at his own reflection. Still, now. Mouth closed. Jaw tight.

That wasn't him.

It couldn't have been.

The platform was far. The light was bad. The angle was off.

There are tall Japanese guys.

Plenty of them. Especially the younger ones. And the suit? Everyone wore suits. That was the whole point. Uniformity. Anonymity. Of course, most wore navy blue but regardless, suits.

You've been in this country long enough to stop imagining shadows.

He closed his eyes. Behind the lids, the bunraku puppet collapsed again. The legs folding. The jerking shoulder. That perfect, helpless fall.

He flinched, snapped his eyes open.

No. Not again. Not here.

He stood and moved toward the exit, pressing the button just before the next stop. The doors opened.

He stepped onto the platform and out of the system.

The city air hit him like a low note.

Not hot, not cold, just full.

He walked fast, then slowed. Took a hard left. Crossed at a yellow light. Zig-zagged through narrow streets with no names. Past shuttered offices, past restaurants setting up for the evening, a man wheeled a cart of empty Asahi crates across the wet concrete, the bottles clinking like glass teeth.

He kept looking behind him, casually, he told himself. Not panic. Just awareness.

No one was there.

Of course no one was there.

But he couldn't stop scanning.

Reflections in windows. Movement in glass. A man on a bicycle riding slow, he watched that one until he turned a corner. Nothing.

The farther he walked, the tighter the streets became. Older. Quieter.

He passed a wall of hand-painted signs, most of them chipped, and a row of wooden slats that formed the outer fence of a small temple.

He didn't mean to stop. His feet did it for him.

Inside the open gate, a monk sat cross-legged, head shaved, shoulders still. A bowl in front of him. His voice droned low and steady, a mantra looping endlessly into the dusk.

He didn't understand the words, but the tone vibrated in his teeth.

Something about it felt wrong. Not malicious. Just *invasive*. The sound wasn't being made so much as emitted, drawn from the air around them, not the monk's throat. The tone fell on him like a prophetic requiem for the coming doom.

He stepped away.

Fast.

He ducked into a corner shop that smelled like fish and old paper. The bentos were cheap and wet-looking, but he didn't care. He grabbed one with pork, a side of noodles, and a soft egg folded like a rag.

Paid in silence. Didn't wait for change.

Back in the apartment, he sat on the floor.

He poured warm sake from a bottle that had been sitting near the fridge vent. Didn't bother heating it properly. Just enough to numb the edges.

The bento was cold. The noodles stuck together. He chewed anyway.

The chant was gone. The train was gone. The puppet, no, *that* wasn't coming back. Not tonight.

But the man on the platform...

He took another sip. Then another.

"That wasn't him," he said aloud.

It didn't help.

Chapter 25: Kaishaku's Feast

The rain hadn't stopped, just changed shape, no longer sheets, but a soft mist that seemed to hang in place. The city lights smeared across wet pavement in long amber strokes.

He'd wandered longer than usual, following his nose more than his feet, until he found it, a narrow stairwell beneath a red paper lantern, glowing softly behind a curtain of drizzle.

The sign said nothing in English. Just black ink brushstrokes on weathered wood: 石蔵. He didn't need to read it. He could smell the broth from the sidewalk.

Inside, the noise met him like warmth. Not loud, just *full*.

Chatter. The clink of glass. A fry station sizzling behind the counter. Someone laughing too hard at something that wasn't funny. It was the kind of place men came after work, jackets off, ties loose, slouched over grilled skewers and shared ashtrays.

The floor was old wood, dark with polish and years of spilled sake. The walls were warm-toned plaster, half-tiled in black. Lanterns hung low. Everything glowed.

He was guided to a small two-top against the side wall, close to the kitchen, away from the front windows. Perfect.

He slid his coat onto the chair beside him. Took the towel he was offered and wiped the mist from his face.

The laminated menu was dense with characters. No photos. He picked something at random, grilled mackerel, he thought, and a side of cold tofu.

The waitress smiled, bowed slightly, and moved on.

He sat back.

The noise was comfortable. It wrapped around him like a blanket.

At the table beside him, two salarymen were deep into a bottle of shochu, laughing over something on a slip of paper. A younger couple whispered between bites, legs tangled beneath the table.

The smell of grilled fish, sweet soy, vinegar rice, it pulled memory from the corners of the brain and replaced it with something simple: presence.

For the first time in days, he let himself settle. Not relax, he didn't trust that word anymore, but *settle*.

The beer arrived, cold and perfect. The foam just right.

He sipped.

Let the warmth spread.

And for a brief, traitorous moment, he believed he was alone.

***

The food was halfway gone. He ate slowly, chewing each bite like it might be the last calm thing he'd get all week.

The izakaya buzzed with afterwork energy, half-lit lanterns overhead, bursts of laughter from tables packed shoulder to shoulder. Oil hissed behind the counter as a cook flipped yakitori over a flame. A warm, harmless place. Anonymous.

He was just lifting a skewer to his mouth when he heard it.

Thump. Drag. Step.

He froze mid-motion. His eyes darted toward the sound.

Thump. Drag. Step.

From the entrance, a waitress led a man down the narrow aisle. He moved unevenly, lurching slightly left with every other step, like one hip was built wrong, or reassembled without instructions.

The man didn't glance at anyone as he passed. But his height, the awkward gait, the stiffness in his shoulders, he knew.

It was him.

The waitress motioned to a two-top two tables over. The man paused. Looked around. Then, slowly, deliberately, turned his head.

And tipped his hat.

A stiff, genteel gesture. Two fingers, a slight nod.

The man felt his spine lock.

Big Shoe took his seat without a word. His coat folded awkwardly at the shoulders, like it had been tailored for someone broader, someone younger. He set a small, worn case on the table, black leather with a brass clasp. Unsnapped it with care.

Inside: a pair of thick, polished metal chopsticks, lying in dark red velvet.

He removed them gently, like holy relics.

Then, never breaking eye contact, he unfolded a napkin. White. Crisp. Began to wipe them down, one at a time.

Not once. Not twice.

Over and over.

Back and forth. Between his thumb and two fingers. His movements slow, obsessive. Like he was preparing surgical tools before an operation. Or weapons before a war.

The man couldn't move.

A flood of adrenaline surged through his chest. His ears rang. His body screamed to run, to stand, to shout, but nothing happened. He just sat there, chopsticks still in his hand, cooling in the air.

Big Shoe finished polishing.

Placed the napkin across his lap.

Then, finally, looked away.

His food arrived: grilled beef over rice, pickles, miso. The waitress bowed and retreated. The sound of other diners faded, as if muffled behind glass.

Big Shoe picked up the metal chopsticks.

And began to eat.

Not like a man enjoying a meal.

Like an animal returned to feeding after being caged.

He tore into the beef with practiced, mechanical bites. Lips glistening. Grease collecting in the corners of his mouth. The chopsticks clicked against ceramic in perfect rhythm, not a single piece dropped, not a single movement wasted.

He chewed with his mouth open, exhaling through his nose in slow bursts. When a bit of sauce dribbled onto his sleeve, he didn't wipe it. Just kept eating.

Faster.

The man couldn't breathe. He gripped the edge of the table, knuckles white. His entire body tensed. He wanted to scream. Stand. Throw something. Anything.

But all he could do was watch.

Big Shoe lifted another piece of beef.

Then he placed the piece in his mouth. Smiled. Silver tooth flashing once in the low lantern light.

And kept eating.

Then, finally, he looked away.

A second waitress appeared. This one was older, quiet. She placed a lacquered board on Big Shoe's table, smooth, black, gleaming in the low light.

The eel was still moving.

It thrashed once. Then again.

In a motion so fast it felt rehearsed, the cook approached. White coat. Thin knife. A pair of small nails.

Tap. Tap.

The eel was nailed to the board through the head. Still writhing.

Then, with surgical calm, the cook sliced it lengthwise. Blood beaded along the flesh. Entrails slid out, steaming. The ribs cracked with a wet crunch as the knife worked down the spine.

The man could hear every detail, the ragged sawing, the wet slap of guts hitting the board. Someone at another table murmured in appreciation.

Big Shoe didn't look at the eel.

He looked **at** him.

And smiled.

The silver tooth caught the lantern light like a blade.

Slowly, still holding that grin, he picked up one of the metal chopsticks. Raised it. And mimed the same sawing motion the cook was making, right in the air between them.

Back and forth. Back and forth.

A slow dissection.

The man's legs locked. His breath hitched. He felt the skin behind his ears go ice cold.

Big Shoe looked back down.

Began to eat.

***

He couldn't take it anymore.

The taste of his own food had turned to chalk. His palms were slick, heart thudding so loud he feared the whole room might hear it. He stood, fast, and nearly knocked over the chair behind him.

Big Shoe didn't flinch. He swallowed a final bite, audibly, then reached into his coat and drew out a fat, folded wad of yen. No wallet. Just a stack of bills banded with something red.

He threw it onto the table beside the half-eaten food and the still-twitching eel carcass. A small pool of blood had formed on the wood beneath the cutting board.

The money landed with a wet thud.

The server bowed, confused, murmured something. Big Shoe didn't acknowledge her. He was already rising.

The man was halfway to the door, weaving through the tight corridor between stools and coats and chatter, when he heard the heavy scrape of the other chair.

He didn't look back. Just moved faster.

Then, a voice. Low. Precise. Almost gentle.

"Leaving so soon?"

It wasn't loud. But it *landed*.

He hit the noren curtain and pushed through, out into the crowd and the noise and the pulse of Friday night Shinjuku.

The air was thick with cigarette smoke and grilling meat. Laughter rang out from a group of students nearby. A salaryman stumbled past with his tie around his head. Neon signs flashed kanji and cartoon mascots across every window.

He turned left, not thinking, just moving.

Then he heard the door swing open behind him.

Footsteps.

Heavy.

Deliberate.

Chapter 26: The Gauntlet

He moved into the street, fast, but not running. Couldn't run. Not yet.

Kabukichō throbbed around him, neon signage stacked in layers, lights blinking like a seizure warning. Pachinko bells, laughter, a thousand overlapping conversations. Drunks swayed under awnings, women in heels barked drink specials from doorways. Taxi horns. A low, rattling bass from somewhere deeper in the maze.

He kept walking. Eyes forward. Elbows tight.

Behind him, the noren curtain flapped once.

Then again.

Then footsteps.

Not fast. Just… sure.

He risked a glance over his shoulder.

Big Shoe had exited the izakaya.

He was moving at full speed now, not running, just walking *hard*, and that's what made it worse.

He towered above the crowd, a full head taller than most. The weird yellow-brown suit, funeral-curtain fabric, caught the streetlight and made him look jaundiced and sick. His foggy left eye caught reflections at odd angles. His black leather glove was off now, stuffed into a pocket, and the large hand hung free, fingers pale and thick, bent slightly inward like they wanted to curl around something.

But it was the gait, the *gait*, that turned stomachs.

That wild, irregular lurch. Like a marionette with one string pulled too tight. His torso twisted side to side with each stride, as though something inside him was broken and grinding.

He didn't dodge anyone.

Every few steps, he collided with someone.

A man in a white dress shirt tried to pass, muttered "*Abunai na*"— but Big Shoe's hand rose like a priest giving benediction, cupped the man's jaw in one grotesquely tender motion, and shoved him straight to the pavement.

The man hit with a gasp. Rolled. Didn't get up right away.

Big Shoe kept going. No pause.

The crowd absorbed it, like a city swallows everything.

The man ahead, the scammer, cut right, deeper into the alleys. Past a host club. Past a storefront selling novelty watches. Past a sign for 3,000 yen karaoke.

He zig-zagged, trying to break line of sight. Ducking between vending machines and crates of empty beer bottles stacked six feet tall. He passed a teenage couple leaning into each other, a woman on a cigarette break adjusting her wig in the reflection of a car window.

He glanced back again.

Still coming.

Still fast-walking.

People parted around Big Shoe like a clot passing through a blood vessel.

No one stopped him. No one even *really* saw him.

He cut left into a narrower passageway. Less light here. Wet concrete. Pipes overhead dripping condensation onto rusted A/C units.

A cat bolted across the alley.

He turned again, a hair salon, closed. A massage parlor with frosted windows. A shuttered ramen shop.

Footsteps. Close now.

The scammer's breath hitched. He reached for his pocket, no knife. Nothing. He wasn't armed. He wasn't even sure if running would work.

But his legs started anyway.

He sprinted.

Shoes splashing through puddles. Dodging trash bags. The sound of his own panting bouncing off the walls around him.

He burst into a wider street, streetlights overhead, a row of lanterns swaying slightly in the breeze.

And then he stopped.

Dead center in the crosswalk, gasping, chest heaving.

No sign of him.

His pulse roared in his ears.

Nothing. Just the dull buzz of the lanterns and the hum of a pachinko parlor nearby. He turned his head, scanned both ends of the street, no sign of the suit, the gait, the eyes. Nothing.

The crowd had thinned. Less noise now. Fewer lights.

He moved again, fast but careful, weaving between salarymen, couples, a cluster of girls with shopping bags. Slipped past a vending kiosk, ducked through an alley marked by a rusted parking sign and a pair of broken umbrellas.

The path narrowed. His shoulder brushed brick. Then concrete. Then tile.

Every turn led him somewhere older, a little darker, a little quieter. Neon gave way to dull yellow bulbs. Modern buildings turned to weathered wooden doorframes and stained stucco walls.

He glanced back.

Still nothing.

He took a side street marked by a crooked lantern and a blue sign with faded katakana. It bent left, then immediately right, like a spine out of joint.

Here, the air changed, damp, close. Trash bins lined the walls, and the concrete was slick with something that glistened but didn't reflect.

He stopped. Listened.

Just the distant sound of traffic.

Maybe he'd lost him.

He moved forward again, slower now. Trying to stay small.

The alley twisted, led deeper. He passed a closed shop with a sun-faded awning. A pile of cigarette butts overflowed from a rusted coffee can beneath a broken drainpipe, like an altar to boredom.

Then, he stopped.

Not from sound. Not from sight.

Something in his chest went cold.

He wasn't sure why.

He turned around.

Nothing there.

Still, the pressure didn't ease.

He took a breath, wiped his forehead. The sweat had gone clammy. His shirt clung to his back.

Another block. Then he'd circle back to the main road. Find a cab. Or a police station. Or something.

Just keep going.

But with each step forward, the alley behind him felt closer.

Tighter.

Alive.

He turned the corner, fast.

Too fast.

A blur of movement behind him, and then,

A sound.

Not loud. More like... a breath. A hiss. The glint of something silver.

And then pain, sudden, perfect, total.

He froze mid-step.

A sharp, alien pressure bloomed just beneath his left shoulder blade. Not a stab. A **pierce**. Clean and surgical. Like the needle of a giant syringe, or a spike through insulation.

He gasped.

But no air came.

His lungs seized. His knees buckled. His head spun.

He reached back. Fingers found a thin metal rod jutting from his ribs, a chopstick. Steel. Slick with blood and already growing warm from his body heat.

He turned, or tried to.

Big Shoe stood just behind him. Silent. Close. Too close.

His glasses fogged slightly at the edges. His lip curled upward, not quite a smile, more like a tightening of the face.

The gloved hand reached forward again, palm pressed flat to the man's chest.

And then—

Push.

The chopstick drove deeper.

He staggered forward, eyes wide, mouth open in a silent scream. The ground lurched. The walls leaned in. The alley spun.

He collapsed to one knee.

Big Shoe just watched. Calm. Precise.

The scammer crawled. One hand. Then another. Blood hit the concrete in fat, wet smacks.

He looked up. A flickering bulb above a rusted door. It blinked twice, then held.

A cough wracked his frame, wet, red. He spit and it splashed on his palm. He looked at it, dazed.

He slumped.

Big Shoe approached. Slow.

He crouched beside him.

Pulled the metal chopstick free with one smooth motion. No flourish. No cruelty.

Just silence.

Then, gently, wiped it clean with a white cloth.

He stood.

Tucked the chopstick back into his jacket.

As the man struggles to breathe, Big Shoe stands above him.

"Und the kings of the earth, and the great men…"

He spoke softly, almost kindly.

"…hid themselves in the caves and in the rocks of the mountains."

A pause. Then —

"And said to the mountains and rocks, 'Fall on us…'"

He leaned down, just enough for the man to hear.

"'…and hide us from the face of Him.'"

The alley began to spin. Blood soaked his shirt. He tried to speak but could not.

His vision fades.

Chapter 27: Hospital Reflections

The first thing he heard was the steady click of metal wheels on linoleum.

Then fluorescent light, too white, too clean. A thin curtain. The sting of antiseptic in his nose. A fan oscillating somewhere overhead.

He blinked. Then blinked again.

Pain blossomed in his side like a tide coming in, slow, then sudden. He tried to sit up, but his body said no. A tube ran into his arm. His shirt was gone. A monitor beeped quietly behind him.

He wasn't dead.

Not yet.

A nurse noticed his eyes open. She pressed a call button. Moments later, a doctor arrived. Polite. Professional. Spoke English passably. Said he'd been found in an alleyway, barely conscious. Said the puncture just missed the heart but collapsed the lung. Lucky.

Lucky.

They asked his name. He gave a fake one. They didn't question it. Foreigners got hurt all the time in Kabukichō. Knife fights, muggings, bad deals. They nodded and wrote it down.

No police came. No forms. Just quiet care and a bill he'd never pay.

He stayed four days. Didn't talk much. Ate the rice and fish they gave him. Watched TV with the sound off. There were bars on the windows. Not for security, just standard issue. Still, they felt appropriate.

On the last day, he stood at the bathroom mirror and peeled back the bandage. The wound was neat. Clean. Surgical. Like everything else Big Shoe did.

He put on the clothes he came in with. A nurse handed him a form. He scribbled the name he'd given. The signature looked like someone else's handwriting. He left before the ink dried.

Chapter 28: Last Call

The payphone felt colder than the night air.
He cupped the receiver with both hands, as if holding it tighter might keep something in, or keep something out.
The smell of cigarettes clung to the cord, to the buttons, even to the dull black plastic pressed against his ear.
He punched in the numbers from memory, watching each digit light up in tired green.

It rang twice.

She answered with his name, not the fake one, not the cautious tone she'd used on other calls. Just his real name, bare, like she'd been waiting for it.

"It's me," he said.

Nothing for a moment but the faint static on the line. It wasn't quite silence, there was a hiss in it, like the air in a sealed room.

"Jesus," she finally said. "You sound like hell."

"I'm leaving Tokyo."

A pause. He could hear movement on her end, maybe the shift of her chair, maybe her crossing a leg over the other. He imagined her kitchen light spilling across the floor, the phone cord stretched over the table.

"Where to?"

"Florida."

Another pause, longer this time. "Why?"

He let the question sit. His eyes drifted to the flyers plastered on the inside of the booth, peeling corners, taped-over numbers, bright images dulled by years of grime.

Host clubs. Massage parlors. Room rentals by the hour. All the ways to be someone else for a while.

"Because it's the end of the map," he said. "And I'm tired of running in circles."

"Is this about him?" she asked.

The question hit like a pin slipping under a fingernail.

He didn't answer. Not directly.

"I can't explain it," he said instead. "Not in a way that makes sense."

"I think I get it," she said. And maybe she did. Or maybe she just didn't want to keep prying at something that made her skin crawl.

There was another silence. Not awkward, not exactly, more like both of them were listening to something else in the room. For him, it was the faint whistle of wind curling around the booth. For her, it might have been nothing at all.

"I don't know if I'll call again," he said.

"That's up to you."

He thought about telling her that he'd been found in an alley with a collapsed lung. That the wound was clean, surgical. That no one in the hospital had asked questions. That the bars on the window weren't for keeping people out, they were to keep people in.

He thought about saying his name aloud, the real one, in case she ever had to identify him.

Instead, he said nothing.

"I'm not coming out there," she added. It wasn't cruel — just plain. "I can't do this anymore."

"I know."

"I mean it. I'm done."

He almost smiled. Not at her words, but at how familiar they sounded. He'd heard that same tone from strangers, from bartenders, from people who'd once owed him something but decided to cut their losses.

"Okay," he said.

The word landed flat, like a coin on wet pavement.

She sighed then, slow and quiet. Not exasperated, just tired in a way that made him feel older than he was.

"Take care of yourself," she said.

"You too."

He waited, listening for the click of the line going dead, but it didn't come right away. For a few seconds more, they just stayed there, two people breathing into a line stretched halfway across the world.

Then it was gone.

He stayed with the receiver in his hand long after the dial tone started.

Long enough for the booth's fluorescent light to buzz and flicker, and for him to wonder if maybe the sound was coming from inside his head.

Finally, he set it back on the cradle.

The metal cord twisted on itself and slowly unwound.

207

He stepped out into the street, the cool air hitting the place under his ribs where the stitches pulled tight. The city smelled like rain on concrete and engine exhaust. Somewhere in the distance, a train moved, not fast, not slow, just steady, the way something moves when it knows exactly where it's going.

He didn't.

But he knew where he couldn't stay.

Chapter 29: Florida (Slow Decay)

He went by "Buddy" now.

The name had come from a waitress, middle-aged, bleached hair, voice like gravel, who'd asked what to call him when he showed up for eggs and toast three mornings in a row.

He shrugged and said, "Whatever's fine."

She'd smiled without looking up from her notepad. "You look like a Buddy."

And just like that, he was.

The diner was two blocks from his rented room, a peeling stucco building with a rust-stained window unit and a warped front door that stuck when it rained. The kind of place where the landlord was seldom seen. Inside, there was a ceiling fan that ticked when it ran, which was always. The bed sagged to one side. The tiny fridge made gurgling sounds when it defrosted. The window unit struggled to attain a comfortable temperature.

But the location was quiet.

And that was worth everything.

He'd arrived in a small fishing town at the edge of the Everglades nearly six months ago, off a Greyhound that smelled like vomit and off-brand cologne, a rolling chariot of despair and last chances. No luggage. Just a canvas duffel, scars on his body, deeper scars in his mind, and a single idea in his head:

Solitude.

It wasn't peace, not really. More like a ceasefire. On humid nights, he could smell the wet rot of the swamp in the air. That smell had become strangely comforting, a reminder that no one followed you out this far.

He found small routines. Grocery store on Tuesdays, mostly frozen meals, instant coffee, an occasional bottle of cheap whiskey if he was feeling brave.

On Saturdays, he walked the trail that skirted the swamp. Sometimes he sat for an hour and watched egrets move through the reeds like ghosts in slow motion.

There were moments where he forgot the face.

The foggy lens.

The limp that carved a path through crowds like a scythe.

But forgetting wasn't the same as healing.

It just meant the wound had grown calloused.

Not gone.

He never saw a doctor about the wound. It healed crooked, an off-center scar low on his back. When he twisted wrong, he could feel it pull like a knot tied too tightly.

But the real damage wasn't flesh.

The real damage was silence.

Silence, when he heard metal utensils scrape on ceramic.

Silence, when he caught the scent of something being grilled and felt his stomach turn.

Silence, when he'd awaken thinking he heard something at the window, only to find nothing there but moonlight and curtain shadows.

Sometimes, he convinced himself it had been a dream.

Tokyo.

The restaurant.

The alley.

A fever episode, maybe.

Until he looked down and saw the way the skin puckered at the scar,

like a signature.

He didn't talk much. That suited people fine.

Florida towns had a certain kind of logic:

Don't ask questions.

Don't answer them.

If you're quiet, you're left alone.

There was an old man who fished at the canal every morning. The two of them would nod, nothing more, as one passed the other.

He didn't know his name.

Didn't need to.

The waitress at the diner still called him "Buddy," though she said it less often now. Usually just wrote down his order without asking.

Two eggs, soft. Toast dry.

Black coffee.

No small talk.

No questions.

He hadn't spoken to his girlfriend in nearly six months.

The last call had ended with the cold silence so long it became its own kind of answer.

He told himself she was safer this way.

A rustling in the reeds when there was no wind.

The feeling of being watched on the walk home.

A reflection in the window that took too long to disappear.

At first, he dismissed it, paranoia, PTSD, echoes of Tokyo still playing out in his skull.

But two nights ago, he'd woken with a jolt, heart pounding.

He swore he heard something move outside the front door.

Just once.

Then silence.

Still, nothing had happened.

No notes. No phone calls.

No gloved hands. No silver tooth flashing in the dark.

Just… waiting.

And that was worse.

He started walking at night again.

Not far, just around the block, sometimes a little farther. Past the closed bait shop with its sun-bleached window decals, down the overgrown sidewalk lined with palmettos and mailboxes dented from too many years of hurricanes. The air smelled like mildew and motor oil. The kind of stillness that makes your own footsteps sound too loud.

Sometimes he followed the narrow-raised path along the canal, the water black on one side, swamp shadow on the other. Not deep into it, just far enough to feel the hush of the Everglades pressing close, the air damp and still, like a breath held in the dark.

He told himself it was exercise. That the fresh air helped him sleep.

But sleep never came easy anymore.

Sometimes, he'd jolt awake for no clear reason, no sound he could name, no dream he could remember. Just a prickling along his spine and the faint feeling that someone had been standing by the bed a moment ago.

Other nights, it was the air itself that woke him, a sudden coolness brushing his cheek, like a door had been opened somewhere and left ajar.

Once, he thought he smelled damp wool inside the room. Another time, a whiff of something metallic. Both gone before he could be sure.

He told himself it was nothing. Drafts. Old building smells. The swamp breathing through the cracks.

By morning, the feeling was always gone, or buried deep enough to pass for gone. But it left something behind, like the echo of a word you can't quite remember, or the shadow of a shape you never really saw.

He began watching the people more closely.

The man fishing by the canal, was he there longer than usual? The woman at the diner, had she paused too long before saying "Buddy"?

He knew how stupid it was. How insane he sounded, even to himself. But the feeling wouldn't leave.

It wasn't that Big Shoe was coming.

It was that Big Shoe had never really left, not the man himself, maybe, but the space he'd carved out in his head, a permanent corner where dread lived rent-free, replaying every attack in slow motion, over and over, until the memories felt more real than the nights they'd happened.

Some days, the weight of it sat quiet, like a storm far out at sea. Other days, it pressed close enough to taste. It was the kind of presence you couldn't walk away from, because it walked with you.

That night, he left the diner later than usual. He didn't say goodbye.

The walk back felt longer. The road looked unfamiliar in places, like the shadows were angled just slightly wrong.

Halfway home, he stopped.

The wind had changed. A moist gust swept in from the Glades, smelling of brackish decay and something else, heavier. He sniffed once. Again.

His hand drifted to the scar at his ribs, fingertips grazing it like a nervous habit. It didn't hurt, but it felt warm. Alive.

He turned around.

Nothing behind him. No one. Just the empty road, power lines humming quietly overhead.

Still, he couldn't shake it.

Something had shifted.

A pressure in the air, like before a storm, the kind that makes dogs whimper and radios pick up static.

That night, he locked the door, then pushed the dresser in front of it.

He left the light on.

Didn't sleep.

And for the first time in nearly a year, he whispered a name out loud, not to summon it, not to curse it, but simply to feel it in the air again.

"Big Shoe."

Chapter 30: Final Pursuit (Everglades)

The moon hung low, swollen and yellow, not full, but full enough to cut sharp shadows along the start of the swamp trail.

He walked without a flashlight. Hadn't needed one in months. His eyes had adjusted to the dark, and besides, there was something about the way the moonlight hit the sawgrass, it made the world feel still. Empty. Like the edge of something.

The Everglades seemed subdued tonight.

Not silent, but different. A few frogs clicked in the reeds. The occasional splash of something unseen disturbed the water. Crickets chirped, but only in patches. As if even they were being cautious.

His boots squelched against the damp edge of the trail. Not far off, the path turned to wooden planks raised above the swamp, but he didn't plan to go that far. Just to the bend. Maybe a little past it.

He told himself this was the last time.

He'd been restless for days. Something electric under his skin. Dreams he couldn't quite remember. That sound again, not the tapping, but heavier. Like breathing behind a closed door. Flashbacks of the silver tooth. the fogged eye, the sickening gait. Permanent residence of his subconscious leaked into his daily thoughts.

He needed air. Space.

He needed to know he was still alone.

The path narrowed as he moved deeper.

The brush thickened on both sides, curling in like ribs of an animal long dead. He liked this part. He slowed his steps. Took in the weight of the dark. Let it press against his skin.

Then he stopped.

There. Ahead.

A ripple in the water.

It could've been anything, frog, gator, even a turtle. But it wasn't the splash that made him freeze. It was the reflection.

A shape. Human. Upright.

Just for a second.

He stepped back. Blinked. The water calmed.

Gone.

His fingers curled. Palms damp. He glanced over his shoulder. Nothing behind him. Nothing obvious.

Still, he turned around.

Started walking back.

Ten steps in, he heard it.

A footfall.

Not his.

Then another.

Closer.

He spun. Raised his hands. Saw only trees and water. Empty boardwalk. Pale moonlight.

Then, there. Just past the bend. Inside the tree line.

A figure.

Tall.

Head just above the grass line, like it always was, like the whole world was tilted slightly in his favor.

The shoulders.

The brown suit.

The staggered walk, but faster now. Urgent. Violent.

Big Shoe.

He ran.

Didn't look back. Didn't breathe right. Just *ran*.

His boots slipped on wet patches. Caught on roots. He slammed shoulder-first into a tree, nearly fell, caught himself. Kept going.

Past the old drainage pipe. Past the part of the trail where the reeds closed in on both sides.

His heart felt like it would break his ribs.

Behind him, nothing yet. No voice. No footsteps.

But he didn't trust it.

He knew the rhythm by now.

It always started with silence.

He veered off the trail. Into the brush. The ground sucked at his feet, pulling with each step. Branches whipped his face. Thorns caught his sleeves.

Still, he moved.

Faster than he thought he could.

His lungs burned.

Then, open space.

A clearing.

He stumbled into it. Chest heaving. Legs twitching.

He spun. Listened.

Nothing.

No footsteps.

No shape in the trees.

No—

A twig snapped.

He turned and ran deeper into the abyss.

His breath came in ragged bursts.
Tree limbs clawed at his face as he tore through the
underbrush, half-sprinting, half-lurching, branches
whipping his arms, sweat stinging his eyes.
Behind him: nothing.
No footsteps.
No rasping breath.
Only the pulsing thud in his own ears and the slap of
his boots against wet earth.

He didn't dare stop.

The moon was high now, pouring silver across the
swamp like spilled mercury. Shadows moved the wrong
way. Insects shrieked as frogs groaned somewhere
deeper in the brush.

He stumbled through a tangle of cypress knees and
vines, panting, heart hammering.
Water sloshed past his calves. Mud sucked at his feet.

He didn't even know where the path was anymore,
if there ever was one.

And then.

His left foot didn't come up.

He yanked. Nothing.

The right foot followed. Deeper this time.

"Shit—"

He shifted his weight and felt it sink.

The ground gave like custard, peat, muck, quicksand,

whatever the locals called it, but all he knew was that it was taking him.

He froze.

His hands shot out to a nearby root, just out of reach.

He lunged for it.

Slipped.

The earth gurgled as it accepted more of him.

Waist deep now.

Cold. Thick.

A vacuum, pulling downward.

"No. No—"

He twisted, reached for something solid.

There was nothing.

If felt as if the swamp was watching the whole display unfold.

He screamed.

It didn't carry far.

He clawed at the muck, tried to dig himself free, only sinking faster.

Up to his chest.

Then just below the ribs.

Then.

A rustle.

He snapped his head toward the sound.

Branches moved.

A figure emerged.

Slow. Deliberate.

Big Shoe.

Outlined in moonlight, suit clinging wet to his body, the platform shoe slick with black swamp water. He didn't speak.

Didn't smile.

Didn't hurry.

He moved in like a shadow stretching under dying light.

The scammer's arms trembled.

"Help me…"

Big Shoe stopped at the edge of the quicksand. His silhouette flickered in the swamp mist.

The scammer's mouth shook. "Please—"

Voice breaking now.

"Help me. You win."

Silence.

Big Shoe's gloved hand extended.

Paused.

Then reached down.

The scammer grabbed it with both hands.

It was cold. Immovable.

Big Shoe pulled.

Hard.

The muck groaned, resisted, then gave.

Inch by inch, the man emerged, slick and shaking.

The swamp spit him out like a rotten seed.

He collapsed at Big Shoe's feet.

Sprawled like something unstrung, face half in the moss, chest heaving in wet, arrhythmic bursts. His arms gave out beneath him. One twitch, then stillness. The night air clung to his skin like silt, thick with rot and memory.

He didn't speak. Couldn't.

Behind him, the quicksand pool bubbled faintly, already smoothing itself over like a wound refusing to scar.

Big Shoe remained motionless.

The man searched for something in that face, even a flicker. Anger, satisfaction, contempt. But there was nothing. No heat, no recognition. Just the kind of emptiness you couldn't bargain with. And that, more than pain or blood, seemed to signal the end.

Then came the sound, soft, deliberate, of the velvet case being unlatched.

The flap opened with a sigh.

Inside, the pick rested like a relic: polished, slender, exact. The glint of its metal barely caught the moonlight beneath the dense canopy, but it was enough.

No words were spoken. No final curse or whispered warning. Just the stillness of a verdict long understood.

And then—

A single sharp cry.

Wet. Truncated. Gone before it could fully rise.

The silence after wasn't peace.

It was the marsh closing in, soundless but deliberate, as if sealing a vault. The trees seemed to lean inward. The frogs fell mute mid-croak. Even the cicadas strangled their own static, the way a record needle lifts before the last note.

Not in pity. Not in protest. But in complicity.

The swamp would take him.

It would drink the blood that pooled in the moss. It would ease him into the black water, where skin would loosen, where bone would soften and sink. There would be no marker, no trace. Only the slow work of rot, carried out in the quiet patience of still water.

For a long moment, nothing moved. Even the air seemed to hold its breath.

Then, drop by drop, note by note, the world began again.

A faint drip from a fern. The gentle pop of bubbles in stagnant water. A distant hoot, slow and measured, from deep in the mangroves.

Big Shoe didn't look back. He knew the work was done, finished with the precision of a man who never left loose ends. He stepped away without hurry, the swamp already folding itself over the scene.

Alone now.

The shut case, held loosely in one gloved hand. His other arm hung still at his side. The platform shoe squelched faintly with each step, waterlogged and heavy, yet his pace never broke.

A figure born from shadow and purpose, he limped toward the edge of the tree line, not rushing, not hiding, only returning.

The moon caught his face for a moment as he passed a clearing. Unreadable. Expressionless.

He didn't look back.

He never did.

Just kept moving toward the world beyond the swamp.

Epilogue: Her Voice

The road was empty.

Just a ribbon of cracked asphalt winding between palmetto thickets and forgotten lots, the kind of place where even stray dogs didn't linger. One yellow streetlight buzzed overhead, flickering once, then steadied.

Big Shoe emerged from the edge of the swamp like a shadow detaching from the trees. The suit clung damp to his frame. Each step squelched faintly, swamp water bleeding from his soles, but he moved without hesitation. No hurry. Just momentum.

At the corner stood a payphone.

It hadn't been used in years. The metal was pocked with rust, the plastic casing yellowed like old teeth. But it still worked. The dial tone moaned to life when he lifted the receiver.

He held it to his ear.

Slid a card from his coat pocket.

Punched in the number.

Waited.

Two rings. Then a click.

A voice, uncertain, soft, answered:

"Hello?... Hello?"

His fingers tightened around the receiver.

Silence stretched between them.

"Hello? Who is this?"

Still he said nothing.

His eyes drifted shut.

227

The streetlamp caught in his eyes. For a moment, he wished he could tell her, the thing that had hunted her was gone now, left to rot, sinking in the black water.

He closed his eyes, let her voice echo for one more second.

Then gently replaced the receiver.

He stood still a moment longer, hand resting on the cradle.

Then he opened his coat.

Inside, the velvet case was waiting, tucked neatly beneath the lining like an heirloom. He ran his thumb along its edge, then pulled it free. Stared at it.

A long breath escaped through his nose. Not relief. Not grief. Just finality.

Across the street, a green dumpster leaned crooked beside a shuttered gas station.

He walked to it.

Lifted the lid.

Paused.

Then dropped the case inside.

No ceremony.

No sound.

Just gone.

For a moment, he stood there, the black leather gloves still damp from the swamp, the fingers stiff with old blood. He peeled them off slowly, one at a time, and let them fall in after the case.

And turned.

The road ahead was long and flat. No cars. No breeze. Just the soft thrum of crickets resuming their song, as if nothing had ever happened.

He walked off into the silence of the night.